Hagit the Israeli

A NOVEL

I0525094

HAGIT THE ISRAELI

A Novel

NAPHTALI HOLON

TouchFeather
Odessa ♦ Seoul ♦ Bangalore ♦ Cebu

Hagit the Israeli: A Novel

Copyright © 2013 by TouchFeather

Paperback ISBN-13: 978-1-59689-116-6

Write-To Address:

TouchFeather
P. O. Box 126
Odessa, DE 19730
The United States of America

Library of Congress Cataloging-in-Publication Data

Holon, Naphtali.
  Hagit the Israeli : a novel / Naphtali Holon.
      pages cm
  ISBN 978-1-59689-116-6 (pbk. : alk. paper)
  1. Americans--Israel--Fiction. 2. Americans--Egypt--Fiction. 3. Travel--Fiction.
4. Love stories. I. Title.
  PS3608.O49435655H34 2013
  813'.6--dc23
                            2013012844

This book is dedicated to my Israeli friends

Chapter 1

That which was to seal my fate was something that evaded me until the very last second. Then, all became crystal clear. A life lived in oblivion or in unconscious waste may be described as pitiful. But such a description would belong to the onlookers. To the one experiencing the fact, all is real and all is gravitas.

One fine day in June, I ambled across the long stretch of a pathway, which was crowded by pedestrians. It was a hot and sunny day, which makes reality appear as a dream. The heat can almost be seen and touched. There is a type of autonomous activity based on habit that takes cruise control. And you are left wondering what is happening. This fine day in June was a fine summer day, and as summer days go, it was a very hot day.

I walked along in my polo shirt and shorts. When I looked around, there were people in pants, and this puzzled me. I guess my American sense of summer could not fathom why people on leisurely walks would put on a whole length pants to suffocate their legs, when the heavy summer warmth was oppressive.

I walked trying to ignore the haters of the summer spirit, towards my favorite spot in the whole stretch of street: the ice cream stand. My favorite ice cream was pistachio, because it looked nuclear but tasted sweet. I guess that is why I liked Israeli women. They were like sabras, they say in Israel; tough on the outside, but sweet on the inside.

I thought about the sweet sabra I knew in Israel. We had met one day, not unlike this day, a summer day. But the Mediterranean sun scorched your skin, not like the northern European sun, which just teased you to death with sweaty heat. Israel's heat was dry, at least in Jerusalem. And it was intense, like the beauty of a red-blooded sabra.

I saw her one day sitting across in a room in the Russian Compound. The popular young Israeli hang-out place was filled with sabras. Hardly any English could be heard. And that's what I liked about the place. Heck, I did not go to Israel to speak English and hang out with fellow Americans. I went to Israel to meet Israelis, especially real live sabras who deserved that title.

At Russian Compound, it was a pilgrim's haven for those who sought sabras. Israelis have a saying, "Your eyes are bigger than your stomach." And this aphorism especially applied to me, whose eyes seem to grow bigger and bigger with one sabra after another. I don't know what it was about these sabras. They drove me crazy.

Yes, it might have been the scorching of my brain cells by the intensity of the Mediterranean sun, especially since I refused to don any oaky hats which numerous guidebooks recommended. But I felt the beating of my heart as not one induced by many dead brain cells, but by my desire to be near sabras and get to know them.

Luckily for me, I had befriended an Israeli friend. I guess he was desperate to meet American women, whom he considered "easy" or "easier than sabras." He thought that befriending me was the way to achieve his Nirvana, a heaven filled with more American women than he could handle. Whatever his motivation, I felt that the fortune was mine, because I knew that any society other than America was not easy to penetrate. If my Ivy League core curriculum taught me anything, it was that people tend to congregate along the lines of "like likes like." And I did not look like an Israeli, not at all. Perhaps, that is why I was such an easy prey for Dodi, who was on a quest of his own.

I don't like to compare his quest to my quest. I feel that my quest is nobler, like a quest of a pilgrim who is after some deeper truth. Just call me, Buddha!

Dodi's quest was more superficial in nature, more carnal in content, and more basic in purpose. Sometimes, I despised him for his crass worldview and goal in life. But then, I needed him. And need creates the most strange of bedfellows. And here I was in Russian Compound with Dodi, who seemed profoundly unhappy that there were no easy catch.

"You just want a helpless bambi, all naïve and innocent, wanting to experience everything," I chided Dodi.

"Nu! What's wrong with that! You live once and then you die. You gotta enjoy life before you die!" Dodi replied.

"I love you like a brother, Dodi, but where did you pick up sorry ass line like that?" I retorted.

"Hey, hey, hey!" Dodi feigned indignation. "Who ya calling ass?"

"No, I didn't call you an ass," I said sheepishly. After all, Dodi was a tough guy. He had scored 97 on the Israeli Defense Force test, which he insisted was a perfect score. I might have doubted the veracity of that claim, but I sure as hell did not doubt that Dodi could go all crazy on me. He was one crazy dude.

"Haver, we are wasting time," Dodi said. "Haver" is modern Hebrew for "friend."

"Come on, Dodi," I said. "We have been sitting here for what five minutes? Give it time."

"Done that. Seen that."

"Geeze, you are becoming more American by the minute," I said.

"I have my sensei to thank for that," Dodi laughed.

"Let me ask you," I interrupted his moment of glibness. "Should I just walk up and introduce myself to a sabra?"

"You are so desperate," Dodi said in his Israeli matter-of-fact manner.

"No, I am not," I said. "I just want to meet some sabras."

"Do you want me to introduce me to my sister and her friends?" Dodi teased.

"Yeah, that would be cool," I said naively, thinking that his offer was in earnest.

Dodi started to laugh out his words, "Ah, you sucker!"

I looked at him with puzzlement.

"My sister is like 15, a baby," he said.

"15 is not a baby," I said. "But I get your point."

"You are going to find out what a real sabra's like," Dodi said with a wicked gleam in his eyes. "Yeah, I dare you to go up to a sabra and introduce yourself."

"You dare me?" I said, feigning anger.

"Yeah, you American chicken," Dodi said seriously. It hurt a bit.

"Okay, my Israeli friend," I said, "I will show you what the home of the brave produced."

"All talk!" Dodi continued to tease.

I got up, as his teasing actually energized me. Fueled by the taunt of my Israeli so-called friend, I walked straight up to a beautiful sabra, not really feeling the ground beneath me. It was too much to think about whether the ground below me existed or not, so I just walked on as if I were walking on water, like in the Gospels.

"Hi," I said, and to my horror, the sabra threw me a smirk. "My name is Pete." I extended my hand for the sabra to shake.

The sabra looked at my hand as if it was afflicted with leprosy. Maybe I was not tough enough like an Israeli, and she looked down at me with scorn. Perhaps, she thought that I was a wimp, extending my hand, when I should have been grabbing her and giving her a Gone-with-the-Wind kiss? The moment seemed long. And the seconds dragged on like the clocks in Salvador Dali's paintings.

"I am from America, and I just wanted to meet an Israeli," I said. Honesty is the best policy after all.

"Isn't that guy over there an Israeli?"

I looked toward the direction of her finger-pointing. She was pointing at Dodi. These Israelis are like hunting dogs. They can smell an Israeli and an Arab from a mile away. Anyhow, how did she know that I was with him? She must be in the Israeli secret service or something.

"Him?" I said, trying to look for words. "He's not Israeli!" I lied out of sheer panic. I felt my encounter with her slipping away, and I just panicked.

"Be-met?" the sabra said, looking amazed. She must have been shocked that her Israeli canine sense failed her. I felt a bit guilty for playing tricks with her mind. It was like toying with your cousin's pet dog and spraying his favorite toy with hair spray. But it had to be done. I was not going to miss out on a chance of my life time. She looked like a model, you see. And I had dragged myself all the way here. It was probably never going to happen again in a million or gazillion years. I had to take the chance when it was so close.

I used her seconds of disorientation to go in for the kill.

"I like the way you look," I said.

She looked up at me with those killer canine eyes. They seemed like the eyes of a fuzzy snow-ball doggy, when she's mad. They looked so cute, a bit out of place from her voluptuous womanly body that was hard and curvaceous, certainly well-toned, visibly.

"I just want to get to know you," I said.

The secret agent ma'am seemed to respect my courage.

"Sit down!" the sabra ordered. I obeyed her like a dog just out of intense dog training school.

"So, what's your name?" I asked.

"My name is Hagit," she said.

"That's a really pretty name," I lied. It actually resembled barfing violently, but I feared that saying the truth would get me shot. I noticed the M-16, next to the chair.

"Todah!" she said, like a soldier woman.

"So, you are in the military?" I asked, stupidly looking at her machine gun.

"Yeah," she said. "You know, we can't leave these things lying around, anywhere."

"6 months in jail?" I said, trying to brag about my knowledge of Israeli culture.

"Oh, you know so much, American boy," the sabra said.

"I try," I said. "But you can teach me far more about your culture. Don't you think that it's your duty as a member of the Israeli military establishment to make alliance with friendlies, such as I?"

She looked at me and laughed. "You are funny, Pete."

I felt like I had an "in." I felt exuberant and yapped away like a young boy on his birthday after blowing out the birthday candles.

She looked at me talking and smiled. I think I was getting to her.

"Give me your hand," Hagit said. "Here's my number. Call me and we'll go out and have fun."

Then, she left. I looked at my hand with a bunch of numbers scribbled on it, and I was in a state of daze. Did she give me her number and ask me out on a date?

I hopped back to my former seat with no shame. I did not care who was watching my victory hop. Okay, it was not one of my proudest moments to hop, like in a hopscotch of an all-women entourage. But make no mistake about it; I had triumphed. Everything else seemed inconsequential.

Dodi looked at me and said, "You are hopeless, Pete."

What did he mean by that?

Anyhow, we quickly finished out Maccabee Beer and thumped out of that one room social space.

"Whereto, bud?" I said with aftertaste of sweet victory.

"Let's go to the Underground," Dodi said. "There are always so many American women, there."

"Ah, you and your quest for the Guiness Book of World Records," I said.

"Hey, I am a man of purpose," Dodi said in his feigned masculine voice.

When we went inside the underground, it was filled with Israelis and not Americans. Dodi seemed a bit disappointed, but he seemed to like the music and started to dance. I started to dance in front of him, and thought that it was a bit gay, so I started to move a bit around the dance floor. One thing about Israelis is that they are homophobic, like the rednecks in Alabama. And that suit me just fine. I had my fill of guys pinching me in a London club, which I did not know was a gay club. At first, I just thought that the club was filled with lonely and shy guys and gals who were dancing with the same sex. Then, it dawned on me around 2 or 3 AM, when these shy gals and guys started to do things. Then, I realized that it was the guys who were pinching me and not the gals. After that trauma, I always made a policy of asking if the club was gay or not. For a straight guy, a gay club can be a traumatic experience.

Israelis did not like homosexuals. Maybe it's because of its military culture. Maybe it was their religion. But I liked the fact that the whole country was homophobic. I felt safe. No fear of some tough tennis players or wrestlers pinching you and leaving you a traumatized bruise or two.

I looked around the dance floor, and I could see all the scantily dressed Israeli women. They did not drink much. I noticed Israelis did not enjoy being drunk. Maybe it was the control thing. Maybe, they feared that if they became drunk,

13

they would not see a Palestinian coming from behind and stabbing them in the back. I don't know what it was that kept them sober in party settings, but I am sure many a mothers in America would like to learn their secret for their teenage daughters. Statistically, many women lose their virginity while being drunk. They don't even know what happened to them. What a tragic way to lose anything, with no memory of whether it was good or bad.

Israeli women were dancing, and everything was bouncing around. They were bouncing around in an athletic way. Not the jello wriggle, that could be nauseating. I was mesmerized by so many scantily-clad Israeli women dancing in synchronicity. They seemed like muses. Their soft skin glistened under the disco lights. Their skimpy tank-tops seem to be lonely and begging for attachment. Their undulating hips seemed to me like the waves of the Mediterranean Sea that sucked you in with each cycle. I felt myself being dragged deeper into the sea.

My brain said, no, but my feet dragged themselves toward the undulating waves in hormonal consent. Soon, I was alone in the midst of waves clashing against each other. I felt the undulating bodies skimming my body parts and felt a sensation of titillation at the points of touch. I closed my eyes in sensual contemplation as bits of thoughts attacked my mind with unsavory thought.

I extended my hand to one of the Muses flashing her belly button, and she responded by holding my hand. I turned her round and round, like a record playing a tune of Lionel Richie.

"Say you, say me, say it together, naturally."

I drew close to her body after a few rotations. Her 19-year old body seemed limber yet firm under my arms, and she pressed closer and closer into me. We danced fast music like it was the slowest music on earth, and felt the earth spin without rotation in togetherness. I could feel her massive womanly figure press against me as if making indents in my body. And I felt a rush of pleasure hit my head and my every other extremity. I felt a type of sweet tenseness in areas that I did not know I could feel. And she wriggled tightly against my body as if she were reaching for her sweet tenseness or release.

I stroked her back as she spun and accidently stroked her front torso and felt the powerful waves that undulated on her body and felt the powerful undulation of my own body. Like a blind man, who could not see, I caressed her body vertically with both my hands as I allowed my hands to explore the full undulation of her body in full movement to the music. Slowly, I raced my hands to her hair and stroked it. They felt luscious and fluffy under my hands. And I touched her sweet cheeks and chin. I drew her lips closer to mine and kissed her on the lips.

The loud music blended with the beating of my heart, and I could see that other areas of my body were beating loudly as well. Her lips felt soft and moist, and then I felt the rush of her tongue into my mouth. And I felt the entanglement of our lips lead to higher levels of sensation and pleasure.

Then, abruptly, the nameless girl with firmly undulating waves on her body was pulled away by a force that seemed to be a very important part of her world. It was her best friend, lonely and alone, who had no surfer to bodysurf on her waves. It was a lonely sea without a ship to ride the waves and to push fishing rod deep into her body of bottomless sea. The lonely, dark sea conjoined with the sun-warmed sea in tumult, pulling it away from its ferocious appetite in the hot, blue sea, with the intense ship stroking it, fast and furious, with its passionate body.

And the ship was left alone in the deep sea, away from the exciting, undulating waves. Just calm and serene. Forlorn and cast aside. And there I was, feeling what I now missed. And my whole body ached for something more, something further, something deeper. And I felt a strange sensation ring silently throughout my body as if my body needed SOS. First aid. Mouth-to-mouth resuscitation.

It was a strange aching that I had not felt before, and the whole newness of it scared me. It was a type of soreness that was a good soreness. It felt good. But it felt painful. It was a new sensation that made me feel alone and empty. It was strange. I felt like I had gained something, but also that I had lost something. It was a sensation difficult to describe in words, but all too real. I felt a keen sense of reality hit me, and it was unsettling, a bit.

But I wanted more. I wanted much more. And my body ached and ached for it.

Chapter 2

It was strange how time passed by so quickly in Jerusalem. Maybe it was the warm summer sun that made everyone feel like a napping kitten on the porch without a care in the world. Everything seemed slower, but in fact, days moved by very fast.

I tried my best to concentrate on my Hebrew. I wanted to become more fluent in modern Hebrew. But, the way I figured it, the best way to become fluent in Hebrew was by speaking to an Israeli. So, I decided to ditch the Hebrew classes and take a road trip with an Israeli. No. It wasn't Dodi. The idea of traveling with Dodi for an extended period of time made my stomach churn for some reason. Instead, I enticed a sabra to make the journey with me.

I figured that it was not really cheating on Hagit, my real love, the love of my life, since she was in the military, and she was on duty for at least another year. She was beyond my reach. Untouchable. Besides, we had not officially become an item.

Anyhow, it wasn't like I was cheating on anyone, since I was not asking the new sabra to be my girlfriend. I merely asked her to go on a journey with me to Egypt. To be completely honest, I don't think she was interested in me, *per se*. I think that password was "Egypt." Maybe I am not giving myself enough credit. People do say that I underestimate myself. One of my female friends had said to me once, "Pete, you are a dangerous man."

Shocked, I nearly jumped out of my seat. "What do ya mean?"

She laughed when she saw me in a panic. "No, it's just that you destroy women."

"Yeah, right," I said. "You are just too funny. Ha, ha."

For some reason, she did not laugh. She merely said, "I have to hit the john." And she disappeared that day. I always assumed that she had the case of the runs.

I had actually posted up an ad on the board by the library. "Hebrew speaker needed to practice Hebrew. Preferred: Female student, aged 20 to 22." Surprisingly, I received the call the very night. I guess that was the benefit of being in a country filled with Hebrew speakers. There was little demand and a lot of supply.

"My name is Hadas," she said. And she was the prettiest little thing that you could imagine. She was 5'2" or so, and she was really fit. Surprisingly for an Israeli, her skin was milky white. She must be one hundred per cent Ashkenazi. I did not necessarily prefer short women, but I wasn't choosing a girlfriend, I told myself. I just need to practice Hebrew and see a little bit of the area, while I was here.

"My name is Pete," I said, and then I went straight to the point. "This is my offer. I will pay for all your travel and stay in Egypt at the same level as where I am staying, in exchange for speaking to me in Hebrew and helping my Hebrew."

"So, you are saying that you will give me a free vacation?" Hadas asked.

"I guess so," I said. "I figure that we are getting a good deal. You get a free vacation to Egypt, and I get a Hebrew tutor for a week."

Hadas looked down at the floor for a second. "Okay," she said in a decisive manner that was so typically Israeli in nature. I knew I liked the sabras for a reason. There was just absolutely no bullshit with these women. It was probably the military that made them so direct and decisive. And I liked it.

"Okay, then," I said. "Why don't we leave tomorrow morning? There is a bus from Jerusalem to Egypt, leaving at 8 AM. It's like 24 hour bus trip, and we arrive in Cairo, the next day at 7:30 AM."

"Sounds good to me," Hadas said.

"Here's 100 sheckels to buy whatever you need for the trip," I said and gave her the bill. She smiled and said, "Thank you."

"Can you come at 6 AM?"

"See you, then," Hadas said.

After seeing her off, I went to buy two round trip tickets at the Mazada Bus Line office. Each roundtrip ticket cost $110 US, and the border tax was $55 US. I felt better after I had the tickets in hand.

That night, I did not sleep, too well. I was just too excited. I had always seen the pyramids in the photos, but I had always wanted to see them in person. Now, I was going to do that. Although I felt a bit guilty about playing hookey with my Hebrew class, I felt justified that I was bringing my private Hebrew tutor with me. I figured that I was getting the best of both worlds.

Next day came, and Hadas was promptly on time. She was wearing jeans and a T-Shirt, which read, "Proud to be Israeli." I rolled my eyes, I think, because she moved from side to side uncomfortably.

When we boarded the bus, I took the window seat. I guess that I should have asked her if she preferred the window seat. But somehow, being a vacationer from lands thousands of miles away, I felt I had the right to usurp the best spot on the bus. Hadas did not seem to mind. I sat down and felt a rush of happiness flood over me. I smelled the jasmine on Hadas' hair as she turned around to look at the passengers in the back and felt like this was the paradise that I had been looking for. Hadas seemed excited, too.

"Have you been to Egypt?" I asked.

"Yeah, but just to Taba," Hadas said. Taba is on the Egyptian side of the southern Israeli border in the Sinai mountain area, and many Israelis go there for swimming and snorkeling.

"But not to Cairo?" I asked, a bit surprised.

"No," Hadas said with her eyes widening.

"That makes two of us," I said. For some reason, we were not speaking Hebrew, but I did not care. And I guess Hadas was okay with that, too. So, I did not mention it.

Somehow, as I looked at the vast desert surrounding the bus, I fell asleep. I dreamt of Hagit. Hagit and I were at the Tel Aviv beach. In my dream, I heard the flying seagulls and the clash of waves. I heard the shouts in modern Hebrew all around me. Sounds of laughter. Sounds of the beach paddle ball hitting the paddles. And I heard the cars honking by in the nearby distance. But all the din around me faded away into the background as I beheld Hagit in her awesomeness. Hagit was wearing her bright, florescent pink bikini. Her tanned body glistened in the sun the way waves of the sea shine like bright stars under the noon-day sunshine. Drops of water cascaded down her long, dark, mysterious hair to her shoulders and down the smooth tanned back only to face resistance at the string tied in a knot of the bikini top that seemed like it could be come undone at any moment. The knot was loosely made. A slight pull would unbind the knot. A small tap would bring the whole armor down, crashing to the ground. Even a weak pull would undo the covering. And the scantiness of her swimwear promised more, so much more, than what was visible.

The visible beauty of what is seen portended the bewilderment of what is unseen. What was visible to the eye was a shadow of the reality. The reality to be revealed would be sheer ecstasy. Like a man having gone without water for days in the desert, then finding an oasis, would the naked reality revealed be. I admired her shielded reality and the revealed form as she closed her eyes and enjoyed all that water cascading down her body. I wondered if she felt each drop as it made its way downward on her very smooth body. I wondered if she could feel the drops of water tracing their presence all over her naked form. I wondered what it would be like for my finger to trace the route of the drops of water, falling down all the way from the crown of her head to the bottom of her buttocks as she sat on that sand.

I wondered if she felt the sand beneath her, holding her up, so that she might display her mesmerizing form. I wondered if she could feel each grain of sand, sticking to her bottom, exposed and refusing to let go. I wanted to confess to her, right then and there, that I knew how the sands of the Tel Aviv beach that was underneath her felt. Or rather, I wanted to tell her that I wanted to feel what the sands of the Tel Aviv beach that was underneath her felt. But I told her neither, for I had been stricken dumb as she glistened in the sunlight. She was like the medium through which the sunrays were extended. She was the representative of the sun who made sun worshippers of us all. I wanted to confess to her how I felt. I wanted to confess to her what I could not explain that I felt. I wanted to confess to her what I could not imagine I would feel if I could feel. I just wanted to confess to her everything.

I saw her move in the sunlight in slow motion as she extended her face to receive more sun. Drops of water traveled down quicker it seemed. The water drops on the crown of her head sped toward the bottom of her bottom, entering the mysteries unseen, after traveling the smooth vastness of her back.

Her legs were stretched out, half bent, as she sat receiving her sun. I could see the flawless legs before me tanning, being

21

pleasured by the sun. I wondered if she felt the sun caressing her long, beautiful legs. I wondered if she realized that she had given consent to the sun to do what he will, to touch her, to caress her, to let his warm touch remain on her tender thighs. I wondered if she consented to the proximity of the sun, knowing the pleasures it would bring. Or, if she had given into the pleasures of the sun's touch as a type of surrender, a form of desired bondage.

She sat there with her eyes closed, her head tilted toward the sun, with her body being pressed and caressed by the sun. And I knew she felt the pleasures of the touch and enjoyed it, for there was a big smile in her face, even though the sun had turned her face into a shining planet. I wondered what it felt like to be the sun with unlimited access to her body, to her back, to her legs, to her thighs, and all that is seen. And I know that she felt the warmth of the sun, the touch of the sun, even where things are not seen. I wondered if she derived pleasure or happiness from the touch.

And I sat there, wondering, in my dream, looking at her, and feeling the heat in my heart, in my head, and in my body. Burning with desire, I slowly woke up. When I opened my eyes, I was leaning against the window. I noticed right away that Hadas was looking at me. She wasn't looking at me in the face. She was looking down there. And I felt a soreness, there, and looked down. It was visibly extended, and I felt a rush of embarrassment enter my being.

"So, you had a happy dream?" Hadas said coyly. You could always count on Israeli women to amplify your most embarrassing moment with brutal directness.

"Something like that," I said, not wanting to be a sore loser.

"Well, think of it this way," Hadas clearly wanted to extend my embarrassment further. "Now, I know that your vital organ is functioning well."

"And?" I said, a little dismayed. Now, I wanted to put her on the spot.

She fished for words, but she fished some out to my surprise. "This fact may be very important sometime in the future."

Now, she was teasing me, and she was succeeding at thoroughly embarrassing me. To my surprise, I noticed a sudden, involuntary jerk down there. What was that all about?

"See what I mean?" Hadas said, refusing to let that one slide.

"Oh, Hadas," I said. "I don't know if I should hate you or love you." I just blurted out.

"Of course, you should love me," Hadas said, and she leaned her head into my chest. "I am lovable."

"That you are," I said in a shaken voice. In my excited state, her head pressing me was a further agitator to my desire. I felt afraid that my desire was not abating. I felt as if my desire was slowly being transferred to Hadas. I can't explain it, but I felt an intense desire to stroke her face and kiss her lips. And the fact that she just rested her head on my chest did not help matters much. Was she doing this purposefully? Was she teasing me? I was still feeling a bit groggy from my interrupted dream, but I let her rest her head on my chest. And to be totally honest, it did not feel bad to feel her dirty-blonde hair. Hadas was not unattractive, even though she was a little short. I figured that this time around, her short height was her advantage. I would imagine that for a tall girl to rest her head on my chest in that tour bus would have been nearly impossible, although I have to confess that I have seen amazing acrobatic feats in women before, even women who are not trained in acrobatics. So, perhaps, I should not speak, too quickly.

"Now, it is my turn to have a happy dream," Hadas looked up at me without departing her head from my chest. "Okay?"

I felt a pang of desire shoot through my head. The fact that she wanted to rest her head on my chest was an aphrodisiac. And her desire to have a "happy dream" in that position made the aphrodisiac intensify its power. I began to desire her with the desire from the dream. She had cunningly stolen my desire away from Hagit. Was that really possible? Was it possible for a woman to steal the desire of a man for a completely another woman, who does not resemble her at all? Could it be possible that a man could be so shallow as to transfer his deep, personal desire from one girl to another in such a split second? Maybe it was just I, who was so shallow. Maybe I was the scum of the male species. Other men had evolved further, and they would not relinquish their claim on a beauty upon whom they had showered their deep, personal desires. But certainly, I came to know myself better that day. I know that the desire that I had for Hagit had mysteriously transferred to Hadas. And I began to desire her with the same passion.

Her sweet-smelling hair was just below my nostrils and that might have been what set my bearing askew, if I were to defend myself. But I had no desire to defend myself or to ask her to remove her odoriferous bush from beneath my olfactory organs. I desired to smell her hair. I desired to be drunk on the smell of her hair. I took a deep break, taking all the odoriferous aroma in my nostrils that I could, the way actors in TV coffee commercials do. And she smelled better than even the best coffee that I had ever smelled. I felt a bit cramped and uncomfortable, but I did not want to move because I liked having her head rest on my chest in that precise combination. She had found my sweet spot, and I felt sweet all over. I felt sweet on her. I wanted to shower her with all kinds of sweetness. I wanted to brush her hair with sweetness. I wanted to plant kisses on her face with my utmost sweetness. I wanted to touch her bare arms with sweetness. I just wanted to be sweet towards her. I just wanted to inundate her with my sweetness. I wanted my sweetness to be glued to her like superglue.

I felt the slow breathing and knew that she was asleep. Here, she was, a stranger. And she felt comfortable enough to fall asleep on the chest of a complete stranger. She felt safe enough to do that. I wondered if her sense of security derived from what she perceived as my vulnerability. She had seen me in my extended state, so to speak, and saw what men desire to hide from friends and strangers alike. And she had exploited my weakness and capitalized on my embarrassment to her satisfaction. I felt naked, utterly humiliated. And she knew that. Maybe that gave her a sense of power. That made her feel that she had dominated me. Maybe that made her feel liked she owned me.

I could not really complain, because sitting there on that bus in the middle of the Negev desert, rushing toward Egypt, with the odor of Israel's sweetest flower bewitching me and a pretty girl leaning her head against my chest, I felt like I was in my Eden. I felt the happiness of Adam before the Fall, when he was cast out into the cruel outside, like the cruel Negev Desert that I saw outside the tour bus. Was Adam able to see outside of the Paradise? Did he understand what he would lose in the Paradise Lost? I understood, because I could see the desert all around me. Without life, or much life. Without vegetation, or much vegetation. At least to the naked eye, all the wasteland. Desert without life. I did not want that. I wanted Paradise Regained. Paradise Not Lost. So, I remained still. Absolutely still.

It was then I realized a danger that could create a Paradise Lost. It was like a serpent that could ruin it all for Adam and Eve. It was the serpent that could prematurely exit the Garden of Eden before productive procreation and the pleasures of the whole process. I noticed that her right hand was resting on my left thigh. In fact, she was grabbing onto my thigh, or it felt like it. I cannot say that I did not find her hold pleasurable. In fact, I derived pleasure from it. Much pleasure. But, it might have been too much pleasure. For, I felt the pleasure swell up in my body, especially in the extremity that seemed to be inching closer to her face. It was like a serpent with a venom, that would shoot out at any unexpected moment and poison the poor, unsuspecting victim. It could not be too pleasurable to be stirred awoke by the odor of the venom shot out to replace the sweet odor of aromatic flowers. And I feared that I could not control the serpent within me. The serpent seemed to be inching towards the prey, and I knew that it had to be stopped before it popped its venom in her direction. It did not help that her right arm was grabbing at my left thigh. It too was like serpent, goading. You will not surely die if you eat of the fruit of the knowledge of good and evil. Eat it and see. Maybe you will like it. Maybe your partner will like it. Eat it and see. Let it out. Let your desire out. Let it all fall into place. Let the pieces fall where they may. Let the snake shoot out its venom. You will not surely die.

But I know that the serpent is a liar. I knew that I could not follow the desires of the serpent. I knew that I had to overcome the desires of the serpent, if I were to remain in my Paradise with my Eve. As the bus moved, her serpent moved closer towards me, which caused my serpent to inch closer to her. It was like the contest of the serpents in the time of Moses. Whose serpent is more powerful? The serpent of Moses or the serpent of the Pharaoh's magicians? It seemed like her serpent was stronger, since with each bumpy movement of the bus, it was bringing my serpent closer to expectorate venom, that foul venom, that would shake a fair maiden rudely from her fairytale dream. The outcome was clear when the battle was serpent to serpent, so I had to stop it another way. So, instead of my allowing the serpents to duke it out as would be natural for them and see who will hold out the longest, I interfered and grabbed her snake and placed the head of the serpent that was ever inching nearer my core, away – toward my knee. Her limp snake obeyed my direction and rested its head on my knee. I could see that with the head of her serpent in a safe distance away, my serpent drew back its head from the position of imminent venom attack. The serpent began to relax. I felt the pain of a pull, like a mild muscle spasm. And the slight pain kept gnawing away. But I felt relieved that the snake would not shoot out its venom with its head fully poised and pointed. I knew that the Paradise would not be lost. It was Paradise Regained.

The strain of the serpent-to-serpent battle was too much, and I found myself cast into a sleep, such as when Adam's rib was taken out to create Eve. I don't know how long I was out, but when I awoke, I saw that Hadas was awake and cheerful. She was looking out the window, the window across from our window. She turned around to look at me when she realized that I was awake.

"Sleep well?" Hadas asked in high spirits.

"Yes, actually," I said. "Did I miss anything?"

"No, not much," Hadas said. "Oh! You did miss miles of beautiful Israeli desert."

And when she saw that I was disappointed, she said, "But not to worry, because it looks just like that." Hadas pointed out the window. I glanced at the outside, and it looked exactly like the desert scene before I fell asleep.

"Oh, you are teasing me," I said. She smiled back and looked adorable.

"So, do you have a boyfriend?" I asked inadvertently.

Hadas looked at me for a second. "Not really."

"What does that mean?" I asked.

"I had a boyfriend, but we broke up," Hadas said.

"Does he know that?" I asked.

"What a peculiar question!" Hadas said, looking a little puzzled.

"What I mean is that does he know that you broke up with him? Does he accept it?"

Hadas replied, "I see what you mean. No, he does not want to accept it. He thinks that we'll get back together. But, why did you assume that I broke up with him and not he with me?"

I said in a matter-of-fact voice, "Hadas, because you are so adorable and no guy can break up with you."

"And you know this after knowing me for a few hours?" Hadas said in a half-serious tone. She was an Israeli sabra after all.

"Yeah," I said slowly, feeling like I was getting the third degree. "So, why did you break up with him?"

"I broke up with him because he cheated on me," Hadas said.

"Oh," I said, "That's horrible!" I wanted to let her know that I cared.

"I know," Hadas said. "Why is it that guys don't know it when they have it good?"

"Well," I replied slowly and wondered if I should give her the truthful version or the politically correct one. "It's just that guys are dogs."

"Dogs?" Hadas responded.

"Yeah, dogs," I repeated.

"That's what my mother tells me," Hadas said. "She says that it is the woman's job to keep her guy in a tight leash."

"Well, I hate to admit it," I said, looking slowly at Hadas' facial expression changes. "But guys are dogs." I figured if I separated "guys" from myself in this way, she would think that I was different.

"So, you are a dog, too?" Hadas asked, looking curious.

"Oh, look at the time," I said on autopilot. "Aren't we at the border, yet?"

"Hey!" Hadas exclaimed. "You are trying to change the subject. Are you a dog, too?"

Hadas had a way of reminding me that she was a sabra and that she had no problem putting me on the spot.

"I guess that since I am a guy, I am a dog, too," I said, thinking that this was the most safe reply possible given the circumstances.

"Oh, I guess you are planning to go into politics in the USA?" Hadas said and rolled her eyes.

"Oh, you Israelis roll your eyes, too!" I said. I hadn't seen that for a while, so I thought that Israelis never rolled their eyes.

"Of course, we do," Hadas said. "We roll our eyes whenever we feel that someone says something ridiculous or stupid."

"Oh, gee, thanks," I replied.

"No, I am not saying you are stupid or anything," Hadas said.

"Oh, no?" I responded. "Just ridiculous, huh?"

"Well," Hadas said. "You do have a funny way about you."

"I don't think that's a compliment," I said.

"No, I mean it as a compliment," Hadas said.

I wanted to see Hadas getting out of this one, so I glared at her. She looked away.

"So, how did you find out that your boyfriend was cheating on you?" I asked. I figured that because she was a little off balance, she would tell me the truth.

"I caught him kissing," Hadas said.

"A girl?" I asked.

"No, a dog!" Hadas said in a louder voice.

"Okay, okay," I said. "So, what is this girl like?"

"I don't know her, really," Hadas said. "But they were definitely kissing."

"Where did you see them?"

"In his room," she said.

"How did you get into his room without his noticing," I asked.

"His door was open, so I walked in quietly to surprise him," Hadas said. "And guess what? I was the one who was surprised."

"That's horrible," I said sympathetically. I figured that this was what she wanted to hear. "What was she like?"

Hadas glared at me.

"The evil one," I said to ensure her that I was on her side.

"She is tall and beautiful," Hadas said, and a stream of tear fell on her cheek.

I did not know what to do. I hate it when girls cry. What are you supposed to do in moments like this? Should I reach over and wipe away her tears? Should I give her a hug? Should I give her a piece of tissue? Gee-wheeze, what do you at a time like this?

"Are you okay?" I asked stupidly.

"Yeah," Hadas said, turning away and wiping her face with her hand.

I fished for tissue and could not find any.

"You can use my shirt if you want," I said, like an idiot.

At my comment, Hadas burst out in laughter. Her tears were still steaming down, and there were liquid mucous matter coming out of her nose. I have to confess that the scene was not pretty at all. I felt instantly turned off by all the messiness about her visage. And I was confused at why she was laughing. I was being serious.

"Your shirt is like sweaty," Hadas said, squinting her eyes. I wanted to point out the irony of the situation, but stopped myself. I figured that she would not take it well, so I just nodded like some toy doll, which is made to do that one function constantly.

"You are the best," Hadas said suddenly.

"Well, I try," I said and smiled.

She found some tissue in her bag and wiped her face. She excused herself and went to the back of the bus where there is a toilet. She took her small bag with her. I figured that she was going to fix herself up. I sighed a sigh of relief. Women just don't look good all messy. I just don't like that. Call me shallow or call me selfish, but I say that I am not so different from other men. Men don't like messiness in women.

We men are always messy and around messy guys. One of the reasons why we are attracted to women is that they are neat and clean. It's such a change from the male world. It's refreshing. Being with a well-groomed woman makes you feel special, like you had just come to Disneyland or a 4-star hotel. That's why men prefer women who are well-groomed. There may be some deviants who fall for the sporty type, but most men I know talk about how butch women who do sports are. Men like to date well-groomed cheerleaders; they do not want to date the captain of the woman's hockey team. She's probably a lesbo, most men would say.

Maybe men feel threatened by women who do sports because men feel that sports is for men. It's like men are born with that thought and they guard it throughout their lives. Only sports involving women that men want to see is mudwrestling, because they want to get a glimpse of a naked, flying breast in the mud-slinging contest. But other than that, men want women to be stationary and pretty.

I bet the feminists hate the way men think. But they are bunch of lesbos, anyway, most men would say. Granted, men will play the game. Yeah, we are sensitive to women's struggles. Yeah, we think that women should be equal like men. But when it comes down to it, men are primal and men are chauvinistic. That's just the way men are wired. If the lesbos don't like it, then tough. What if a pretty gal doesn't like it? Well, you know that saying. There are a lot of fish in the sea.

The way I see it, it is impossible for women to win in this world. This is a world dominated by men. Women are at the mercy of men. Men throw women some bones because men don't like the constant nagging and the protests. But when it comes down to it, it is a man's world. A smart woman understands this and goes along to get along.

The women who don't? Well, they can be sure that they will be unhappy, grouchy spinsters with no man to call her own. Owning a man is like owning a cat. You gotta let the cat do its thing and hold onto it only when it is necessary. No cat likes it when its master comes and gets in its way when it is having a cat fight or out roaming the wild with the stray cats. Obviously, locking a cat inside the house is a good way to make sure the cat behaves. So, should the women do? If they don't want their men to stray away, then just lock him in. But obviously, just like with a cat, make sure that you don't make him feel like you are locking him in.

This is relatively simple. Just get a big plasma TV with all the sports and move channels and give him the remote control. You will only see him emerge for food and for bathroom. Men are simple creatures. Problems rise when women expect men to become complex. No, men are simple. Men like simple things. Men can be controlled through simple things. This is the deep truth that women must understand, if they want to be happy.

I figured that Hadas did not understand this simple fact. Obviously, I am not complaining, since one man's loss is another man's gain. But I bet Hadas had a lot to do with why her boyfriend went astray. Maybe Hadas doesn't know how to leash her man. Maybe Hadas is expecting her man to be complex when he is simple. I knew Hadas was at fault. Deep down, I knew. But I wasn't going to utter a word to Hadas about it, because I know that she won't understand. She is a woman and only speaks and thinks like a woman. No amount of reasoning will persuade her. So, I am going to go along to get along. Yes, her boyfriend was at fault. That scum! Sorry excuse for a man!

Hey, I think I got this thing okay. I guess, living in America is a big advantage. Unlike other parts of the world, Americans have to hide our male chauvinism. Yes, women should have equal rights. Yes, women could be just as good presidents. Yeah, sure. Of course! Do you see me protesting?

I wondered what was keeping Hadas so late. She must have been there for like 30 minutes. Okay, maybe it's not that long. Maybe she has diarrhea? I have heard that when you are upset, you can get the case of the runs.

I remember people telling me to be careful about King Tut's Revenge. It's the diarrhea that you have in Egypt. It's not simply diarrhea. It's King Tut punishing you from his grave. I was told that as long as I drank bottled water and brushed my teeth with bottled water in Egypt, I would be okay. Eat food at places where I see westerners. Then, I will be okay.

I felt prepared for this trip to Egypt. I know I was going to have a great time. I have always read about Egypt. And now, I was going to see it. How great was that? And I have this cute Israeli chick to keep me company, and she just broke up with her boyfriend. And she is on the rebound. No wonder why she was leaning her head against my chest. It's the rebound factor working, here.

Yes, she dumped him. But in a sense, she felt as if she were dumped because her boyfriend chose to cheat on her with someone, else. After all, does not action speak louder than words? She dumped him with words, but he dumped her with his actions. Who knows? Maybe he wanted her to see her there. Maybe he had made the call to her to come see him. He probably left the door open on purpose. He wanted to show her because like Neanderthals, men are primitive and primal. They are not in touch with their emotions, and they are wusses about hurting a girl's feelings.

And obviously, being a man myself, I understand. Hadas is such a nice person, who would want to hurt her feelings by dumping her? You would live with a guilty conscience the rest of your life. You would live in fear of bad karma. Every time you walk under a scaffold, you will walk slowly looking up because you would think that bad karma will send a loose piece of wood down and impale you for dumping such a nice girl. Who would want to live with that fear?

No, it's simpler this way. She goes on thinking that she had dumped you, when in fact you rejected her first. But because she thinks that she dumped you, she will think that she inflicted emotional pain on you. Obviously, that's not the case.

The moment she dumped you, your heart leaped for joy, because that's what you wanted. You had calculated to have her dump you, because that was the easy way out.

Can you imagine if she didn't dump you? Then, you would have to go to plan B. And as everyone knows, most men do not have plan B. So, had Hadas refused to dump her boyfriend, he would have become her slave for life. Do you remember when you cheated on me? That would be the password to get whatever she wanted. She could have lived like a queen with total control over him.

You want to go out for beer with your friends? Well, I better come along. Do you remember that time when you cheated on me? What is he going to say to that! The argument is won before it began. The way I see it, Hadas had thrown away her omnipotent power.

I bet the lucky bastard is having the time of his life, right now. No guilt, since Hadas dumped him. The girl who was there and saw everything feels guilty because she thinks that she is the cause of all that pain, and she will bend forwards and backwards to make him feel good. He probably feels like a prince, now.

What did Hadas get in return? Uncertainty. Does he love me? Did he ever love me? Did I do the right thing? Hadas is in a hell that she herself created by dumping her boyfriend. The way I see it, Hadas had given her boyfriend a paradise and put herself in hell. Where was I? I was in purgatory. Hadas saw me as someone through whom she can regain her redemption.

Am I not lovable? Let's try with Pete to see, if I am lovable or not? Can I be a good lover? I want to do all that I could to have Pete tell me that I am a good lover. Am I easy to get along with? Well, Pete will be my proof that I am someone who is easy to get along with.

What does that make me? I guess a type of a god, as far as Hadas was concerned. When it dawned on me that I had this power, I could not but confess that I wanted to abuse it. I wanted to see how far I could push this new power of mine. How far can I go with her? I felt like a bad boy because I was feeling bad and thinking bad thoughts. They were not evil thoughts like maiming a little child. But I did want to take advantage of Hadas. I felt guilty that I felt that way. But I guess that is the natural heart of a depraved man. Power corrupts and absolute power corrupts absolutely. I felt I had power over this guilt-stricken, unsure girl, whose world was falling apart, and I felt a not-small amount of pleasure in it. Does it make me a bad man? I think it just makes me a typical man. What man will not exploit such a power? Such is the depraved heart of a man.

Strangely, I felt a sense of contentment when I realized that I was capable of evil. It was strange, because I considered myself an ethical person. A moral person who cares about what is right and wrong. But somehow, with the fragile girl in the back of the bus, I felt omnipotent. I was wondering how far I could go with Hadas.

"What's that smile you have on your face?" Hadas said.

"I don't have a smile," I protested.

"Yeah, you do," Hadas said.

"No, I don't," I insisted. I knew that the moment I admitted that I had a smile on my face, I would lose my omnipotent power over Hadas. I did not want to do that. I did not want to fall into my kryptonite. So, I kept insisting with the utmost seriousness in my face.

Hadas was sitting next to me. I felt like she was a bit aloof. What was the matter, here? I was a bit confused. She looked straight ahead like a zombie. I looked at her and tried to make sense of what she was thinking. Was she mad at me for some reason? Did I do something wrong?

Then, it struck me. Here was a complex organism much more evolved than the male species who was trying to regain her power over me. She was playing a type of a complex game, which I did not understand. But I realized that I was a part of it.

I was at her mercy if I kept playing. So, I stopped, and leaned my head against the window and tried to sleep. Maybe I will have another good dream. Strangely enough, I fell asleep.

When I awoke, I could not but notice that Hadas was glaring at me. I did not know how to read her facial expression, partly because I had just woken up. I felt groggy, and I did not feel like I had a good bearing of where I was and what was going around. I guess I should have had more sleep the night before, but it could not be helped. We had to take this trip early in the morning, and I was too excited to sleep soundly.

Something told me that something was wrong. Maybe it was the way her eyes had become smaller, more squeezed, that was making me feel that way. Maybe it was that none of her body was touching me. Such a contrast from before! I did not know what to feel.

I felt as if Hadas was withholding her affection from me intentionally and purposefully in order to have me feel it. But I did not feel anything. Certainly, I did not feel pain or sorrow. I did not feel lonely. I did not feel I did anything wrong. But I guess that right thing to do in this situation is to act as if I felt hurt. I dunno, but I guess I will go with that.

"What's wrong, Hadas?" I aked, trying to give the expression that I was hurt.

"You are so cold," Hadas said.

"Me?" I said somewhat surprised by her accusation. "I don't understand."

"How could you turn away from me and just fall asleep like that!"

I did not know what to say. "I am sorry." I remember dad telling me that whenever women accuse you of something, just say that you are sorry, and everything will be okay. For once, I decided to take my dad's advice on women. Well, I was in a half-a-daze, so it was the last resort.

Surprisingly, her tense facial expression softened. And she said, "You don't care about me."

"No," I said. "Of course, I care about you." And I took her right hand into both of my hands and sandwiched it. "I care about you a lot, Hadas."

I felt a bit strange saying this since I had known Hadas only for a day, but then I am a guy and guys lie to girls. So, I was just being a member of my species. To be frank, I dreaded her giving me the fifth degree. I did not want her glaring at me like that. It just felt weird. And men don't like weird.

I stroked her hand and assured her, "I care about you, Hadas." I was lying, of course, but I could see that Hadas was drinking up the cup of lie like some desert wanderer who had journeyed for days on drops of water from her empty water jug, when given a cold glass of water by an accidental tourist.

"You do?" Hadas said, looking up.

"Of course, I do, Hadas," I said. I fished for what I thought she might want to hear. She had just dumped the guy, although really he had played her and tricked her into dumping him. She was insecure and feeling guilty. What should I say next? Obviously, it was clear. "You are so lovable. How could I not care about you?"

I said it slowly since I was still groggy from sleep, but I think it had the effect of making my statement earnest-sounding. It had the desired effect. She drew closer to me, and her right arm began to touch my torso.

I reached out my hand to stroke her hair, like I do with a cute looking cat. She seemed to respond well to this and leaned her head against my chest. I wondered if she knew I was lying to her. I wondered if she realized how ridiculous I sounded saying I cared about her when I had known her for one day. Less than a day.

Then, it dawned on me that she wanted me to lie to her. Maybe she knew I was lying, or maybe she did not. But she preferred that I lied to her, rather than tell her the truth, if the truth was going to hurt her. I realized then and there why the people call women the "fairer sex." It may mean that women are better groomed. But I thought that it means that they are more fair than fair because they will give you excessive amounts of the benefit-of-doubt. If she were fair, then she should have called me on my bluff, on my lie. And that's what men would do. Because men are the "fair sex". But women are the "fairer sex" because they go beyond what is fair. I guess, in this sense, women reflect the mercy of God more than men.

"I care about you, Hadas," I said for another time. I don't know why I said it, again. Maybe it was the overwhelming sense of desire that began to fill my being. The moment I started to touch her hand, I began to feel my desire budding. And the moment that she put her head on my chest, I could feel a burst of desire shoot through my body. I wanted to touch her and caress her and lie to her and tell her how much I cared about her as I caressed her all over.

I wanted to lie to her because I desired her. I guess that I had entered a different stage. I had lied to her at first just to dissolve the tense situation. Now, I was lying to her because I wanted her and her body. Masculine desire had taken over. And I realized that I was too weak because I am a man. Desire for a woman can become encompassing and all-powerful.

I said again, "I care deeply for you, Hadas." I felt weaker, but felt a strange kind of energy running through my body. And I began to believe that I felt like I said. I began to believe that I cared about Hadas.

I don't know what made a believer out of me. But something had happened, and I was believing my own lie. I was believing my own lie as if the earth that I was standing on was actually flat and not round. It seemed like an absolute fact to me. I cared about this girl. I cared about Hadas. I wanted to protect her. I wanted to make her happy. I wanted to be there for her. I wanted to be with her to tell her that all was going to be okay. I desired to be her knight in a shining armor to rescue the damsel in distress from all her unhappiness. I wanted to be the one brave enough, powerful enough to do this.

As I saw her and felt her leaning her head helplessly on my chest, I felt tenderness for her, that I did not remember feeling for anyone else. It felt strange, but it also felt good.

Chapter 3

The border check was gruesome. There were not many people there, but it seemed to take hours. I don't know if it was inefficiency or policy. Maybe they were delaying things intentionally to test the patience of perpetrators that they were trying to block out. Although an innocent man, I felt myself tested. I wondered how many innocent people threw a fit at that border. Were any such innocent persons arrested as terrorists or as dangerous?

The whole definition of who is a terrorist seemed to be shady on many levels. Now, the Syrian and Lybian governments were calling the rebels in those countries, "terrorists." I guess that on one level, they had a point. After all, when a bunch of civilians take up weapons that can kill and use them intentionally to kill members of the ruling government, they could be classified as "terrorists," even by the most conservative political theorists.

The rebels were calling government agents and soldiers, "terrorists." This ironically seemed like stretching the word and the meaning of terrorism. I guess the right question to ask is the question of legitimacy. What makes a government legitimate? Is a government that is elected by the majority vote of the electorate legitimate? By that definition, Adolf Hitler was a legitimate leader, who had the mandate of the people. Would people agree to that statement? Or, is legitimacy based on holding of power? This would include political leaders who are not in democracies, but I would imagine that many people who are concerned with human rights may protest to this definition of legitimacy. Besides, most people feel uncomfortable with pure power becoming the basis of legitimacy. Perhaps, because of the prejudiced perception of the abuse of power that can be the peccadillo of every leader, most people militate against pure power being the legitimizing factor in a leader. But does discomfort mean that we are right? Or maybe, we are uncomfortable, because it is true. We may hate to admit it, but ultimately, it is sheer power that legitimates a governing authority.

Maybe, sheer power is the force behind legitimacy for governments, but sheer power is not necessarily the legitimacy for authority in interpersonal relationships on a personal level. For example, one honors a father suffering from Alzheimer's Disease, even though he may be powerless and may even not understand who he is. Certainly, there is something greater than sheer power that gives the disabled father legitimacy to be honored by a healthy son who is much more powerful than he. One factor that may give the father the legitimacy is natural selection. He happens to be the father, so therefore, he has the legitimacy. Perhaps, there is an unknown natural law operating that orders the universe in such a way that fathers are expected to be honored by their sons. Besides this biological explanation, there might be a religious explanation as well. It is no secret that one of the Ten Commandments demands honoring of parents. The religion that dominates western culture and, in many cases, western individuals order society in a particular way. In the case of fathers, Christianity confers legitimacy upon the father as a matter of principle.

However, does legitimacy function in cases where those who are the governed refuse to recognize the governing authorities, whether they be political entities or one's father? In the case of Adolf Hitler, there was the general consensus of the people, who actively recognized his legitimacy. Although a minority of people protested, the majority tacitly acknowledged his legitimacy to rule, even well beyond the elections that brought him into power. One can say that it was the conscious and proactive support of Hitler's legitimacy as a political and national leader that allowed Hitler to rule basically uncontested until his final demise at the hand of his enemies.

On the other hand, in the case of America, American farmers as well as American patricians refused to support the legitimacy to rule by the British Empire. This rejection of legitimacy caused the American people to rise up to overthrow the British Empire. Obviously, the history shows that American rebels were successful and American terrorism against the British Empire triumphed. Thus, a new ruler was established. And this new ruler's legitimacy was supported by the mandate of the people. But what if the American Revolution had failed? Would the British Empire have continued to rule American colonies? It seems that this could have been the case, when one looks at other commonwealth countries. Does that mean that legitimacy is ultimately guided by power in the case of political rule?

It seems to be the case. Might is right may be applied to modern political bodies, which had been displaced from its traditional and religious modes of thought. Whereas the unit of the family continues, by in large, in the religious axis, or cultural-religious axis, the unit of the body politic, at least on national levels, seem to function on a different, perhaps more confused axis, which is not clearly defined. In other words, power is not the dominant control factor behind the legitimacy of the father, but power seems to be the dominant, although not exclusive, control factor behind political legitimacy.

In this light, both the leaders of Syria and Lybia are fighting for their legitimacy. Ultimately, what will determine their legitimacy is their power-victory over the rebels. If they are successful at suppressing the rebels, then they will, in effect, have legitimacy over their people. However, on the other hand, if the rebels, who from the vantage-point of the state are "terrorists," triumph, then they would wrest legitimacy away from the current legitimate leaders of Lybia and Syria. In other words, legitimacy is for Gadhafi and Assad to lose. In this matrix of legitimacy, it makes sense from the vantage-point of legitimate powers to use torture and secret police and violence to destroy the "terrorists."

This philosophy of guarding legitimacy is nowhere better reflected than in American TV show, "24." The CTU (Counter-Terrorism Unit) uses torture and breaks all rules to make sure that the power currently dominant (the current US government) is not toppled by any rebels, or "terrorists." The TV show "24" tacitly justifies torturing government agents and even killing government agents, loyal to the US government, in order to protect the legitimacy of the current regime in power. Certainly, the TV show "24" espouses use of violence and violation of all human rights laws in order to torture and destroy the "rebels," who pose a threat to the legitimacy of the current regime. Given the philosophical position that might is power, or power is legitimacy, the political and philosophical position of "24" makes sense.

In the same vein, violation of human rights by Gadhafi and Assad, who are still technically legitimate rulers of their countries, are justified and can be seen as the right course of action. In the end, only thing that matters is legitimacy, according to the current political climate and theories. Human rights can be used a s a weapon against enemy regimes to topple them and confuse them from their position of protecting their own legitimacy, but human rights cannot be seen as an operative value for the governing power in the present political climate, both in the USA or in Arab lands. And that is why Hillary Clinton and Barack Obama have had no effect on the legitimacy debate of Libya and Syria. Everyone in the world recognizes that Gadhafi and Assad are playing by American rules of engagement. Thus, American leaders have lost their legitimacy to be the moral voice for the world. By playing with 2011 rules of political engagement, Hillary Clinton and Barack Obama try to assert their moral right to international leadership by show of force and violence. Might is power, and power legitimates.

What will happen to America? It is safe to assume that the American Empire has entered its last phase of existence as an Empire. Just like Greece. Just like Rome. It has reached the end of the period of the Empire, because America lacks power to assert its legitimacy. Every protest against Libya and Syria highlights the vulnerability of America. Weakness is detrimental to legitimacy. Staying out of other people's frays is wise when one does not have the power to assert one's legitimacy. America cannot assert its legitimacy in Libya and Syria, because as Americans say, "We are spread out too thin." Militarily, America's Army, Navy, and Air Force are vulnerable, and everyone in the Pentagon knows it. Politically, America has lost its clout to China. Economically, America is a slave to China. And America's manufacturing power is all but dead. Every time, America meddles in the affairs of other nations, such as Libya and Syria, America's vulnerability is accentuated for all the nations to see. And when there is blood in the water, sharks will come.

Fortunately, Hadas and I passed through the Egyptian border with relative ease. And another bus waited for us to take us to Cairo. This tour bus did not appear to be as advanced and modern as the bus that took us from Jerusalem to the Egyptian border. It was an Egyptian bus with Arabic words written on it. And after the bus started, an Arabic TV program came on in the TV screen at the front of the bus. We would all have to endure the Arabic music being played. But it was not unpleasant. There was a strange, oriental mystique about the songs, that could be described almost as romantic.

This time, Hadas sat by the window, and I sat next to her. I liked this position better because I felt that I could control our proximity better. Furthermore, I felt that I now had an excuse to look at her and pretend like I was looking out the window. I had grown attached to Hadas, and I enjoyed looking at her. But I don't know if she enjoyed that or not. Obviously, I was not going to ask her. I needed a pretext for looking at her, and the beautiful Egyptian desert seemed like just the excuse. Okay, the desert looked eerily like the desert in Israel, but I was not going to volunteer that info.

I felt like a lazy cat, sitting next to her and wanting to sleep. It felt like we had slept the whole ride from Jerusalem to the border. Maybe the bus ride had the effect of a rocking chair that put the riders in a soporific disposition. But the sleep lullaby, as inaudible as it was, seemed to be having its powerful effect. And I fell heavily asleep in a short period of time.

During the short time of sleep, I dreamt about a girl that I once knew. It seemed like such a long, long time ago, although the memory of her cut like a knife, whenever I remembered her. I simply did not understand her or what she wanted. She was a confusing enigma, and that irritated me. I did not want to see her or talk with her, because she was so irritating at times, but other times, she could be so sweet and agreeable. I was wondering why she used this good cop – bad cop routine on me. Maybe, she did not know what she was doing. Maybe, I was imagining the whole thing. I sometimes wondered if I was simply going insane. I felt insane at times, so logically, I figured I might be going insane. But then, I knew that the source of my insanity was none but this little, small girl. How could something so small make so much trouble?

Whatever her weaknesses, I had hard time forgetting the way she looked at me. It is hard to describe, but in her eyes were a kind of puzzlement and wonder. Maybe, I was making her go insane, and that I was just a mirror image of what she was doing to me. But when I looked at her eyes, I could see that there was a kind of trust, a kind of relinquishing of self. She looked at me with a type of complete self-abandon that only showed in her eyes. Nothing in her body belied her blind trust or self-giving. But in her eyes seemed to be a message. A message that she badly wanted to send. That she was desperate to send, but somehow she did not know how to send. There was earnestness and a type of helplessness that betrayed her weakness. It was a weakness that she had voluntarily embraced. And I could see that she was struggling to fight against this. I could see that one side of her wanted what the other side did not want to want. And I could see the fierce struggle hidden behind her eyes. And the synthesis of her thesis and antithesis was desire. Simple and pure. Desire, longing, wanting.

It puzzled me why she looked at me that way. And it puzzled me why she seemed to be so dispossessed by what was running through her mind. She seemed to lack control over something in her mind. Her fiercely independent nature fought to regain control, but I could see that she liked the fact that she had already lost control. She was in something, something she was not familiar with. And the newness of the experience, the sense perceptions, the lack of control seemed to fascinate her. She did not understand it. I could see the puzzled abandonment that signaled me to come closer. But I wasn't sure. I did not trust the message.

What if she is a Delilah? Maybe, she is a femme fatal, who is out to destroy me? Maybe, she has taken out a contract against me. Maybe, I have taken too many *Mission Impossible* movies, but the latest one hit me hard. The one that takes place in Russia, where the director of Mission Impossible is killed by none other than Russian police who are supposed to protect him. Of course, they were under the mistaken impression that he and Mission Impossible had bombed the Kremlin. But that small detail does not detract from the fact of fragility of life. Fragility of power. Fragility of trust.

Why would she want to destroy me? Maybe, I am a megalomaniac who thinks that he has something that could be destroyed. I can only laugh at this idea, because I don't think I am "full of it." But then, I can't really judge myself. Maybe, I am "full of it." Maybe, everyone else around me is saying, "God! He's so full of it!" or "Gage me with a spoon!" Well, the older generation of Babyboomers may say that behind their Republican garbs.

But I felt that there was something not to be trusted about her. I dunno why my innate instinct kicked in and sent alarms. Maybe it's the little things that she let slip, perhaps not knowingly, that gave her away. There was something about her that was not, well, how can I put it....pro-me. Somehow, she seemed to stand for something other than me. I could not put my finger on it, *per se*. And maybe I was being hypersensitive. But I felt that she was batting for the other team. Okay, it is true. I don't know what the other team is. I don't even know what game I was playing. And I still don't know. It seemed like some divine being in his sick sense of humor stuck me in a Death Race, the re-run to the re-run. But it wasn't the cars which were trying to destroy me. But it was like *The Truman Show*. People around me had been contracted to destroy me in creative ways.

Crazy? Yeah, see what I mean. I might have to marry some woman who is doing MD-Ph.D. in delusional studies to steady my being. Or, maybe , I will just write and write and burn my writing after the fact. Maybe, I have seen femme fatal movies, one too many.

I guess, I am a product of my culture. And my culture, being American, is very mistrusting of people. Americans are trusting on the outside, but very cynical and mistrusting in the inside. Even the nicest person in the world will fundamentally mistrust you. I think that foreigners assume that Americans are naïve and that's where they go wrong. Americans only "act" naïve, but they are complex entities with a lot of mental baggage. Despite the European pretensions to sophistication, I feel that Europeans are far more simple, compared to Americans.

The look. I can't wipe that look out of my mind. It's like mites that burrow inside your skin and lays eggs. These mites make your skin look like Klingon foreheads in Star Track. And you have to kill these mites with an all-over-the-body lotion that basically incubates the mites inside your body with poison. What a way to die! I would hate to be a mite, trapped in a human body, waiting to be killed off by an all-over-the-body lotion that some chemical company in New Jersey made. Good to be human. Good to be human, I say.

She looks at me as if she can taste me. Like you can almost taste the turkey stuffing that you smell on Thanksgiving Day. You can just taste it, even before you can see it. And you know that it's going to be yummy in your mouth and in your belly. And you can just taste it. Better than actually eating some food that you don't like, like breakfast cereal that you have had for two months straight, because your mom has become a BJ junkie.

I see her looking at me, and I see that she does not see anything else that surrounds her. And that puzzles me. The only time that I remember a girl looking at me like that was the moment when she asked me to kiss her. She said, "Just kiss me." And she said it with her face like a couple of inches away from me. There was a kind of serenity, like with this puzzlement girl, and her eyes were fixed on me in a similar way. I could see desire in her eyes, and that's really hard to explain. Aren't eyes, just eyes?

But then, maybe I am wrong. I think, I have seen that expression, other times before. I remember the girl who told me to kiss her because she was so blatant about her desire. It's like being hit over the head with a tennis racquet. "Hey, I want you to kiss me!" Bang! Or, ding! However, a tennis racquet sounds on a person's head. I guess it would sound different if you are hit on the head with the string part of the racquet. Obviously, it would be more painful to be hit over the head with the aluminum or Kevlar part of the racquet. But I bet nothing hurts more than being hit with the handle of the racquet.

Could it be that it was the look? The look. But without the commentary or explanation or exhortation. I could swear that I have seen that look on more than a few occasions. I wonder what a woman feels when she gives that look. Does she know that she is giving that look? Does the woman feel desire? Does she feel desperation? Does she feel a tingle in her feet and her bowels, because she feels that she will miss it? Miss the moment? Miss her desire? That she will be left with nothing? Left without the desire of her heart? Left alone, to suffer the memory of being alone? Not having what she really wanted?

I cannot confess to having mite-like skills in going under someone's skin or understanding how a woman feels. And that's why I wasn't sure if this girl was my Delilah. I think Delilah was in love with that prophet from the Bible, Samson. The poor guy! Here, he was, a man of God. A prophet. A judge. And he could not keep his thingy in his pocket. Did he not read his Handbook for Prophets? He wasn't supposed to be cheating on his wife with some Philistine hussy, literally! He was a prophet, for God's sake! I think that the Rule Number 1 for a prophet is: "Thou Shalt Keep Thy Thingy in Thy Pants." Or cloak. Clothes that are covering your body. Kilt, or male skirt. Whatever.

But no. This prophet of God just had too much mojo. He should have undergone that mojo-detraction procedure that

Austin Powers went through. But yep, the story goes that Samson was the wayward prophet. Yeah, he did his thing, but then he let his thingy do its thing. That was the problem for this prophet. And we all know how it ended for the lover of Delilah. Yep, it did not end well. He lost his hair. Then, his power. Then, his eyes. Then, his life. In that order.

That's what I would like to tell all my Sheikh friends who cut their hair. What's up with that? They actually have the excuse to grow their hair and wear that cool hat and carry a dagger as a part of the Sheikh tradition. I was talking with a Sheikh at a gas station in New Jersey. Is it me or are all the gas stations in New Jersey owned by Sheikhs? When I saw a Sheikh without his cool hat, I thought he was a Muslim or something. He had that Arabic look. So, I asked. I hope I did not offend. Just trying to make small talk, you know. But he said he was a Sheikh from India.

I told him. Don't you know the story of Samson? If not, he should read about it. What's a Sheikh with cut hair? It's like a Hasidic Jew without his ear-locks. It's like Moses without his staff. It's like a man without his thingy. It's just not cool. To my surprise, he agreed with me, and said, "It's because the motorists think I am a Muslim terrorist when I wear a turban."

I said, "Oh, please! You just wanted to look cool like Bollywood movie stars. You gave up your Samson powers to look like the Khan brothers of Bollywood. Shame! Shame!" He looked dejected and refused to take the tip. I kinda felt bad, but not really. What is this world coming to, if Sheikhs are cutting their hair to not look like Muslims? Something is very wrong with the world.

And we know something was very wrong with Samson's world. More specifically, something was seriously wrong with Samson's woman. No, not the wife. Remember, he was like the male version of Hester Prynne. Yeah, she had her husband, but she was doing her thang with some holy man. Okay, maybe it's not exactly the same, since Delilah was supposed to be a

Philistine hoe. Yep, Samson was doing the dirty with someone who was not his wife. Maybe that Sheikh guy at the gas station would say, "karma!" at the end of the Samson story.

By the way, do Sheikhs believe in karma? I know that Hindus do, but Sheikhs are shrouded in mystery. A Hindu friend of mine said that they are like Hindus, but they are also like Muslims. What the heck does that mean? I don't see how Sheikhs can be anything like Hindus or Muslims. Sheikhs don't cut their hair, buddy, except the Sheikhs in New Jersey gas stations. So, how are they like Hindus and Muslims? It's not just the hair.

If there is anything I learned from American culture, hair is sacred. Not having hair can be a message. "Be like Mike!" may be one, when we talk about Michael Jordan of the Air Jordan fame. But "I am a skin-head!" can be another message.

Having hair is message-laden, as well. And Sheikhs being required not to cut hair, I am sure, understand the deep significance. And therefore, I bet Sheikhs are different from Hindus and Muslims. It's like the Fonzie of the "Happy Days" fame. His perfect hair dubs him as the cool one, and every woman knows it. Hair is a symbol. Hair can be a diadem. Hair can be related to power. And the Sheikh at that gas station lost his. Dude, you know what you've done! Just to appease some of us white boys in New Jersey turnpike?

What did he think? That a bunch of New Jerseyans are going to spray his gas station with semi-automatic bullets because he was wearing a turban? No faith in the American people. Okay, I guess that's not really an argument. Americans did go in and bomb Iraq, just because they are Muslims. And they did kick out tens of thousands of Muslims or detained them in detention centers with suspended civil rights and legal rights. So, maybe this Sheikh has a point. But then, as a white boy, I can't be bothered. What does interest me is the story of Samson.

Going back to our theme and rumination, hair is sacred, and Samson's power-giving hair was cut because of some hoe. Yep, Samson should have listened to his mom and stuck with his own, then he would not have had his hair cut off. It was like being emasculated for Samson.

Did Delilah love him? Simple minds will say, "No." But every romantic knows and will sing to the soft tunes, "You can't always have what you want." Yeah, you know the song that your grandpa always sings. Yeah, he was young once and, believe it or not, that song was popular for a while. Don't tell Eminem that, because I don't think he has a grandpa, and I don't think he will believe it. Doesn't Eminem think he's black or something? Kind of like Michael Jackson, but in the reverse. Michael Jackson thought he was white or something. But Eminem is better than the Gloved One. Michael Jackson failed to whiten his skin and died looking like a ghost, but Eminem succeeded, unlike Vanilla Ice, to be accepted in the Hip Hop mainstream and among black people.

But let's go back to the hapless prophet. Did Delilah love Samson? My response to that is: "Probably." Hey, women are complex beings. They are like cats. They will love you, but they will let your worst enemy shoot you in cold blood in order to save her own butt. Okay, that may be my misogynous side talking, but don't blame me. Blame the patriarchal, misogynous American society that coddled and fostered me, if you want to blame anyone. But I still think there is some truth to that misogynous statement. And you need to look for truth in everything. How else would we improve as the human race?

But, you can't really blame Delilah for trying to save her butt, can you? You expect her to die herself and let Samson live, so he could go and screw some other hoe? Come on! What universe are you living in? Delilah was probably thinking: "What good is Samson, if I die?" Logic works from a basic biological survival level.

Yeah, Delilah loved Samson. But she wasn't going to die. She had to decide, and she chose herself. You can't expect everyone to be like Hester Prynne. Besides, Hester Prynne is a figment of some male author's imagination. Does someone like that really exist in history? I say not. Girls are cats, and guys are dogs. That's just the way life is.

So, was my Delilah. The one with the eyes. The one with the look.

It was this rumination that I woke up. Pretty strange ruminating in your dream. It's like you standing still and thinking in your dream. Kinda weird. But kinda cool in another way.

I awoke and looked out the window. There were miles and miles of desert. I took out my water bottle and took a few gulps of water. And once hydrated, I gazed at Hadas, and felt genuinely happy. I wondered how I was so fortunate to be sitting next to this cute girl who seemed to warm my life. And I wondered why I was so lucky in life. Somehow, I must have done something right in my previous life to deserve all this.

While wallowing in my good fortune, I remembered my dream and the rumination in my dream. I was not fortunate at all. I wasn't lucky. In fact, I was absolutely cursed. I must have done something bad in my previous life to deserve the punishment of Lord Krishna in this life. There was no Ganesh, the elephant-nosed fortune god, to smile on me. I was absolutely cursed.

I remembered with pain wringing through my heart what I had lost. It was my Delilah. Yes, she was not a figment of my imagination. She was real. She was very real in my life. And unlike Samson, who had enjoyed her and her company and her love. I had not.

I wondered what was worse. To be betrayed by the woman you love after you love her and experience her love, or to not experience the love of the woman you love. What was worse? I couldn't say because I had never felt the first. But I was an expert on the second. Maybe, I was protecting myself and my heart so much from pain, that I was not allowing my heart to experience the limitless potential joys.

I thought about Samson. He had never once complained about Delilah. Samson was no dummy. Samson knew that Delilah wanted to know his secrets, and that secret was going to destroy him. Maybe Delilah was a dumb blonde, and she did not understand what it meant for her to divulge Samson's secrets to his own enemies. Maybe she knew, and she just wanted to protect her own butt. But it is possible that she was a dumb blonde who just did not understand the ramifications. She might have thought that it would all work out in the end.

But Samson knew. That is why he lied to Delilah about his own secret. He lied and lied until she cried and told Samson that he did not love her. "You don't love me, Samson. Why would you not tell me the secret to your power? You just don't love me. You don't love me!" Well, Delilah, maybe it's because Samson knew that you would tell his secret to his enemies and that he would end up blind and dead! Kapish?

But Samson loved Delilah, and he told Delilah his secret because he could not bear her accusing him that he did not love her. That is the man's real weakness, his love. For Samson, it was more bearable to die, knowing that Delilah knew he loved her, than live, letting Delilah think that he did not love her.

How screwed up is that? See! This is how I think. I would say, "Screw, you, Delliah, you fucking bitch! You are fucking trying to get me killed by asking me about my power. You are going to fucking tell my enemies, and I am going to end up dead. Fuck you! Fuck you, Delilah!" Yeah, that's what I would tell Delilah.

I guess it is easy for me to say. I don't love Delilah, and Samson did. To love a woman can be a dangerous thing. To truly love a woman is a dangerous thing, especially when she is like Delilah. Whether she was a dumb blonde or whether she was a selfish bitch, the end result is the same. You end up dead!

Because I can't be like Samson, does it mean that I am not a romantic? Does it mean that I have never been really in love? I dunno. I have no way to judge that for myself. I believe that I have been in love, in real love. But I don't agree with Shakespeare in saying that it is better to have loved and lost than never loved before. I just don't agree with that.

I don't think that there is a soul mate or that a person can only love one person. I think that anyone is capable of loving any number of persons. What determines that you love someone is circumstance and timing. I am sure that there was a time when Samson walked into a bar and saw Delilah and said, "Damn! She is the finest piece of ass in this bar!" And he went after her. She probably played hard to get, and he had to work for it. Maybe not, since she is a prostitute, in terms of her profession, but maybe he had to work for it in order to be her lover. I have heard that it was harder to be a boyfriend of a hooker than a boyfriend of a normal person. By the way, is it true that a hooker will not kiss you, because she is reserving kissing for her boyfriend? Or is that an urban legend?

Anyhow, in the process of Delilah and Samson being together, Samson decided that he really loved her. And it got to a crazy point where he was willing to die to prove that. What gets a man to that point? I have some theories about that. It's not unlike patriotism. What gets a man to a point where he feels he is doing the right thing by throwing away his own life? For a country? For God's sake! Is that ever worth it?

For a woman? Maybe that is worth it? Okay, that's not worth it, either, I guess upon some thought. But at least, you can touch a woman and she gives you pleasure?

For a country? You get nothing, and you lose all. Patriots who willingly die for a country are fools. They are short-changed. They get nothing for their life. But why do they do that?

Well, I figure that people get to a point where they need to believe in something. Maybe, it is due to a fact that they feel that they have done nothing significant in life. It's possible that a person needs to believe in something outside of himself, maybe because he's lived a very selfish life. So, a person says to himself, "I will die for my country, because my country is worth dying for." Is that really an argument? It's not logical. It is illogical to die for one's country. The statement and the logic are circular in nature. Yeah, father or mother dying for their child makes sense. It's biological, and it is natural. But a person dying for his country?

What's a country but a fictional identity? You can't even draw a physical boundary or put a fence around the "real" boundary. The boundary is invisible, and just because you live within this boundary, you can call yourself a citizen of that nation. Okay, there is the plastic ID card. But there is no value in the plastic or the card, except the value that is placed in it by the group of people who live there, who agree to give it value. If one day, all the Americans say that they won't recognize the driver's license as the ID card and police officers say that and all the other people, then your driver's license no longer is a valid ID. It is arbitrary – not just the identity card itself, but the supposed identity that you have, such as the US Citizenship.

In a sense, we are a group of grown-ups, playing this game of life, and we have clubs and club cards, and that's how we determine identity. We make club rules and expect everyone else to follow them. And when people break club rules, we throw them in jail, which we create for the purpose. And the whole human existence revolves around this game that all the adults somehow tacitly agree to play.

It's really stupid. It's really no different from the games that children play. The difference is that adults have better ID cards and better jails and better gadgets and get paid for playing the game of policeman or a judge. And you are going to die for this stupid game?

Are you seriously telling me that a person in North Korea is not a human or inferior to you because he is a Communist and his political affiliation is opposed to democracy? You are saying that a system of political ideology – or, ideas – make you somehow better than them? Come on! You must be kidding me! And we should starve people in North Korea to death because their government does not subscribe to your ideology? What does that make you?

Let's see. You put sanctions on a whole country, knowing that these sanctions will starve people to death. And then the people die, whether it is North Korea or Iran or Russia or whatever the country is. And then, you say, "Oh, those poor people are dying from starvation. We need to help them." Then, you take a collection of few million meager dollars and ship it over to the country. Half of it is taken by administrators in the organization, and only a few people eat for a few days.

Why is there the hunger problem? Maybe, could it be, because you put sanctions on their government and the people? And this is right? Righteous? That God in Heaven likes it when you put sanctions on Iran or North Korea or Russia and then watch them die? Do you think that God is a Democrat or a Republican or supports democracy? God must hate all Communists because you do? God hates Iran, because you do? And you think that you have the right to play God and sanction the nation and its populace to hunger and death.

I think it is poetic justice that Europe is tethering on the verge of death. I see that and see that God is just. Europe wants to impose sanctions on Iran and whichever country that does not agree with it ideologically. In essence, they are murdering people because of political differences. Are there not Christians in Iran? Christians die along with Muslims in Iran because of the sanctions. Don't you think that these Christians in Iran cry out to their God when they die of hunger? Then, Europe, which also worships Christian God – What should happen to it? What will God do?

And look at America. Why are there the problems of housing and unemployment? Is it because there is a poetic justice for all the sanctioning of nations by the USA? United States has killed more people in the world through their sanctions than any other nation in the history of humankind. If God is love and God is just, it stands to reason that God will punish America. So, it makes sense that there is this mortgage crisis in the USA.

And some idiots are going to die for this oppressive and murderous nation? And then, he is going to say that he is upright, and that he died for a worthy cause. You gotta be kidding me!

But people do delude themselves into thinking that it is a worthy thing to die for a country. It is a strange thing. That person might have lived a very selfish life and is looking for a way to prove that he is not selfish. Thus, he joins the Marines or the Navy Seals. He thinks that it gives him value, his life value.

The same kind of stupid logic must go inside of people like Samson, who gives up his life for a woman. I love you so much, that even if you kill me, I will love you. How twisted is that! But Samson lived a selfish life, focused on love and pleasure and satisfying himself. At some point in his life, he decided that he is willing to die for the love of Delilah, because it is worth it. His love is worth it.

It is a strange thing, but people try to find reasons for the value of their existence. And the two biggest culprits are country and love. What hogwash! What has your country done for you? John F. Kennedy, I hear, was an absolute asshole. So, it makes sense that an asshole like that says, "Ask not what your country can do for you, but what you can do for your country!" Kennedy the Asshole Supremeness did not want you to ask what your country can do for you, because if you asked that question, you would think of a million things that your country can do for you. Seriously, what has America done for you, personally? Did America help the poor have equal chance at success as the wealthy? Did America not bail out large banks, which gave multi-million-dollar bonuses for CEO's who are already being paid millions at a time when normal Americans are losing their homes to foreclosure? Really! What has America done for you? Can you tell me one thing that America has done for you?

No. Because America has done jack shit for you. You have done everything for yourself, and you had to fight every step of the way to get there. America has done jack shit for you, and America will do jack shit for you. And you are going to die for this jack shit country? You must be fucking kidding me! But no, Kennedy wanted to keep the poor people down. If Marx was correct in saying that religion is the opium of the masses, I would say that it would be even more correct to say that patriotism is the cocaine of the masses. It looks like sugar, but it aint. It just sends you on a high, and then you become a junkie and lose everything. Your house, your family, your life. Just for that fix. Yeah, patriotism is the cocaine of the masses. And the asshole Kennedy knew it. That's why he said, "Ask not what your country can do for you, but what you can do for your country!" What an asshole, that Kennedy. I hate that Kennedy and all the other Kennedy's who ever sat their fat asses on the Senate or other US government seats. That fucking Kennedy was telling people to not question the government. What an asshole. What? We are supposed to be slaves of our nation? You whup me? Sir, may I have some more, sir? Yessir! Whup me, master! I don't ask what you can do for me, but what I can do for you, master. Whup me!

Kennedy is what's wrong with America. Politicians after politicians want Americans to keep taking that cocaine, called patriotism, and not question authority. Like that would make everything better. Yeah, take the cocaine; the whole world looks better. Patriotism, that's the ticket. Fuck you, Kennedy! May you rot in Hell, forever!

And I say, "Fuck you, Delilah! Rot in Hell, forever!" And maybe that's why I never got together with my Delilah. I was not born into wealth and did not have everything handed to me. And I did not live a life of selfishness, all myself. I had to fight for everything that I received, and I value my life and what I have achieved in my life. And there was no fucking way that I was going to let some sweet piece of ass take that away for me for some sugar. Or some cocaine.

If I cannot trust a woman, then she's done. That's it. I am not going to risk my life and entrust my life in the hands of a woman, any woman! And I hope that I will have the two cents not to trust my wife with my life, when I do get married. I guess that there is less chance of being betrayed by your wife, since you share a common destiny to an extent, but I know the story of Helen of Troy and Paris. Your wife can betray you for some boy-toy. Let's face it. Don't get so full of yourself that you think that no boy-toy can take your wife's affection away from you. You are either over-estimating yourself or over-estimating your wife. Either way, you are looking beyond the mortality and the limitation of humanity. We are humans, and we are not gods. This means that we are fallible and we make mistakes. This means that you can make a mistake, and your wife can make a mistake. No one can be fully trusted, because all are human.

If you recognize the fallibility of humanity, you have a greater chance of living longer and living with your wife until you both die. But if you do something stupid and ignore your wife's fallibility, then you are burdening your wife with information or knowledge that may be too much for her to bear. Is it really fair for you to be that selfish and put undue burdens on your wife? To give her the key to your life and death? That knowledge is too much for one person to bear!

If Samson really loved Delilah, Samson should not have told Delilah about his weakness, about his secret that could kill him. If Samson did not tell Delilah, then he would have been happier, well, because he would not have had his eyes gauged out. He would have lived longer. And Delilah would have been happier because she did not need to see her boyfriend's eyes gauged out. The tragedy is that Delilah probably genuinely loved Samson. But it is too much for one person to bear – the secret to end one's life. It was unfair to overburden Delilah with this secret.

An important thing for human beings to accept is the humanness of humanity. This is why I don't like Mormonism. Mormonism believes that you can achieve divinity. Just call me a bigoted rationalist from the West, but that don't jive with human experience. Show me one perfect human being in the world, and then tell me that humans can become god. Mormons must be fucking kidding me!

Did I love my Delilah? If I had to be honest to myself, I would have to say, "Yes." Do I still love her? Well, what does that mean? Do I think about her? Hell, yeah, especially when I see a room full of ugly women! Do I want to touch her body? Hell, yeah, whenever I think about her! Do I want to hold her in my arms? Hell, yeah, and more! Does my body ache for her? To be honest, not all the time. But yeah, there are times, it becomes unbearable. Is this love? As *Whitesnake* sang, "Is this love that I am feeling?" I dunno. Maybe it's just lust interpreted as love. But if love can be that, then, Hell, yeah!

But I don't think it is worth it to be with her, when I have the suspicion that she is detrimental to my health, mental or physical. "What's love got to do with it?" as Tina Turner sang. That has some truth. Love just ain't enough!

Do I regret not doing more to seal the deal with her? Kinda. But then, if I went further, I would probably be in further agony. That is why I disagree with Shakespeare. It is not better to have loved and lost than not have loved at all. I would say that it is far better to not have loved.

I don't want a Delilah or a Helen or a Cleopatra. It all ended ill for the lover. I want a woman who completes me. Yeah, it is corny. And yeah, the phrase conjures up the scene from "Jerry McGuire," where Tom Cruise says, "You complete me." But she was worth something to Tom. She gave something to him – hope. Something positive. It was a give-and-take. And there was no life-threatening situation involved. There was no risk of losing it all. All the conditions were right for the merger to happen. They were both single people who were eligible, who had something to gain from the union. That is an ideal match. None of this: I like that married woman, and I know that she is perfect for me. Obviously, she is not perfect for you, because, hello (!), she is married!

I think that normal men want two things from marriage. They want a stable woman who can be a good mother who raises his offspring well, since they will biologically carry his legacy. Secondly, they want a wife who will not cheat or betray. Most normal men want these two things from the woman that they marry. I think that love is secondary, no matter how much men may lie and say that love is the most important. Men are logical beings, who act rationally, when they can. Men don't want to get married, so when they do, either they were forced, or they have come to that decision rationally. For normal men, the rational decision would include the above mentioned two factors.

Men distinguish between girlfriends and wife. Yeah, from their girlfriend, men want a lot of things. But those same things, men do not want from their wife. That's what women don't understand. I remember a female friend of mine saying to me, "Love is the goal, and sex is the game." What planet did she come from? No wonder, it is so easy for men to get into the pants of women like that. For men, sex is sex. Men don't really think about love. That's why men don't say, "I love you." Men don't really think about love.

But of course, I would like to think that I am different. Even though I have rationally outlined the nature of man, I would like to say that I am different. I would like to say that I am all about love. I would like to say that I can make a woman feel love more than she has felt ever before. I want to believe that I am the greatest lover, and that women would swoon at the very mention of my name.

I want to think that I was chivalrous and that I would do anything for the woman that I love. That I would climb the highest tower in the land to rescue a damsel in distress. I would like to think that I am a knight in a shining armor.

But I know that I have to grow up and throw away my fairy tale books. There is no good that can come to a grown man, holding a fairytale book.

When I was a child, I thought like a child and spake like a child, but when I grew, I threw away childish things. When I was a child, I thought how square my father was. He wore the same pants and same type of shirt, every day, and went to work early in the morning and came back late at night. All he did was work. And he always restrained from yelling at my mother and tried to agree with her whenever she said something stupid. And I saw that and thought to myself, "What a dweeb! I hope I never grow up to be a dork like that!"

But then, as I grew and saw how my friends had dads making weekend visitations and how my friends were sad at their parents' divorce, I came to understand that my father had succeeded in his marriage, whereas my friends' parents had failed in their marriages. Success is success. And I began to think that my dad was better than the dads who failed at their marriage. If they were so good and so cool, why could they not keep their woman loving them? Obviously, because they were dweebs without mojo who could not keep their woman satisfied.

And as I grew and saw how other families suffered financially, losing their homes and businesses collapsing, I began to see my dad and his hard work ethic as something that was to be admired. I am glad that I did not grow up with a dad who could not keep his marriage together. I am glad that I had a stable home to make me feel safe. I would have hated doing visitation on weekends. There are so many things to do on weekends than being forced to spend time with your father who is not living daily with you, so you have to make the time to visit some stupid place like the zoo when you are in high school.

No, I liked the fact that my dad was always around at my home, so that I could ask him questions about homework or about life, when I needed to. But I also liked the fact that he did not force me to spend one-on-one time with him unnecessarily, like my friends with divorced parents had to experience. We did things as a family and that made me feel secure. The world being cold and seeming to get colder and colder, every day, a stable family was something that I treasured and still treasure.

When I marry, I want to marry someone who can be a good, faithful wife and a good mother to my offspring. As it is, after 30, women start to sag, anyway, no matter how hot they were when they were young. Everything sags, from their breasts to their legs to their belly to their face. Okay, Asian women seem to escape that better than non-Asian women, but it must be some Confucian secret or something. Most women seem to sag, everywhere. And you have to expect that your wife's going to gain some pounds after the children. It's a collateral damage that you have to expect and live with. But then, she will be the mother of your offspring.

A hot woman is a nice thing, but really, most men ejaculate after 15 minutes of intercourse. Most men don't even last that long. And during that 15 minutes, how much is a guy thinking about the woman that he is screwing? Really! For most men, a woman is like trophy. You want a beautiful woman by your side, not really for yourself but for your buddies, so that when your buddies come over for Super Bowl, they will say, "You are a stud, dude! Look at your wife! She is smacking hot!" That's basically why you want a beautiful wife. When you turn off the lights of your bedroom, women are the same anatomically. And when you are screwing a woman, it's not like her vaginal hole feels different because she is prettier than another woman. For God's sake, you know it's about male ego.

And after you fuck the girl, she is going to feel undesirable, even if she is a Victoria Secret model. You know what I mean, if you are a guy. So, a beautiful woman serves only the primary purpose of bragging rights. Yeah, it is a macho, male-chauvinistic thing. That's why you want a hot wife. It's like having a Porsche. But you know that you may not want a Porsche, but a Mercedes Benz. It's more dependable. In fact, a Porsche may make you look tacky at your age. It's not like your 17. At 35, you will look like some cradle-robber with your Porsche. You may stand out in ways that will not be flattering. A beautiful woman can make you look much older, and everyone will be saying, "How old is your dad?"

And if she is thin? You are going to look like Java the Hut. Your trophy may have the opposite effect of making you look absolutely old and decrepit. And you will be there at the Super Bowl, looking like the biggest piece of loser ass in the whole stadium with a smacking beautiful woman at your side. And the moment that the woman of yours throws a smile at some 20 year old? Well, you get the point. The whole stadium may be shouting, "Loser, Loser, Loser!" Or, they may have on the screen: "Look at that loser on row 30, seat five," as they flash your picture and your smacking hot woman inching away from you on the large screen for everyone to see. And people around you will be saying, "Loser, loser, loser!" Yeah, you get my point!

You think that they will fail to see your receding hair line or your beer belly that used to be a six pack, like 20 years ago? It's like Donald Trump with a young beautiful woman. He looks like some old grandpa set in his ways with his granddaughter. And you are expecting him to say, "You are fired!" No, Mr. Trump, this is not "The Apprentice." It's really life, Grandpa! And the girl sitting next to you? Well, she is hoping that someone will say, "You are hired!" And no, Mr. Trump, we are not referring to you.

You see, my dad loves my mother. And they have grown old together, and that is a beautiful thing. When they sit together, you feel that they belong. And no one understands my father like my mother, and he loves her genuinely. And that is a beautiful thing.

I see their wedding photos and see how they were attractive as a young couple. And then, I see the photos of their aging together with us children in their midst, and I think to myself, "Here is a winner!"

Many men today do not understand what it means to live a happy and winning life. Many think that the playboy playmate that they are next to want them for more than their money. They actually fool themselves into believing that they love them. How pathetic have you become, Mr. Trump? And others like him.

When I was a child, I thought like a child. But when I became an adult, I put away childish things. And that is why my father has gone from a dweeb to a stud in my eyes with each passing year.

I cannot honestly say that I will be as successful as my father. The current generation is a cursed generation. Divorce is happening at the rate of 50% and people are damned to unhappiness and loneliness. Maybe, this is partly due to the American government sanctioning countries like Iran and North Korea and killing a slew of poor people in these countries who suffer because of the American-government imposed sanctions. God is taking it personally, because He likes poor people, and God is whupping the wealthy American people with unhappiness by inflicting divorce on them and leaving them painful lashes on their backs.

Yes, I am a part of this cursed generation and this cursed nation. God bless America? Yeah, wishful thinking! That's the best that will be. Say it until you go blue, and you will not see any evidence of that from sea to shining sea. Yup, that's life in the sanction-happy era of America. God bless America. That just makes me laugh, because it is obvious that it just ain't true. Ask any red-blooded American if he feels like God blesses America.

God bless America? You mean like that is why we have over 3 million foreclosed homes? Like that is why our poverty line is going up every year and some 30 million Americans are at risk for starvation? You mean like how America is the fattest nation in the world? Everyone is so fat that guys are finding other guys attractive, because all the women around them are like 50 pounds overweight and their belly is bigger than their breasts or their butt?

It's a curse, man. God must hate America, when I see how fat everyone is. My doctor from Bangladesh tells me that the number one cause of death is obesity. And all the Americans are fat, fat, fat. It's like God hates America and has damned the majority of Americans to a slow painful and costly death journey because of obesity. My Bangladeshi doctor tells me that you can get diabetes because of obesity, heart disease because of obesity, kidney failure because of obesity. He's mentioned a slew of other illnesses, but I forgot, and to be frank, I can't understand him well, because he has this strong Bangladeshi accent. He talks like that guy in the Qucky Mart in "The Simpsons," but a bit different. I think I mastered that Quicky Mart accent, but I can't understand my Bangladeshi doctor, completely. He's so intense. You know these Asians. They are so intense. I rather go to an Asian doctor who speaka no English than go to an American doctor who speaks perfect English. Because you know, an American doctor is probably doing a line of cocaine in his office before he sees you. You can't really trust a white doctor. But you know these Asian immigrant doctors. They are straight as an arrow. I call it compensatory lengthening, meaning that his shortness due to accent is more than made up by his being straight-as-an-arrow as a doctor.

That goes to my next point. God must hate America, if so many people are doing dope. Really. Can you trust a doping doctor? How about engineers and factory workers who do dope? Looking at all those people doing dope in high school and college, it seems like the majority. That's why I don't trust a white doctor. Given the statistics, there is a high chance that a white doc is doing dope. And I don't want no diagnosis by a dope-head. I have heard of people wrongly amputating the wrong arm in a hospital. I am sure that dope was involved somewhere in the chain of command. And you tell me that God bless America? You must be on dope! Yeah, be happy! Peace, man! Groovy, like a spoon! God bless America. Yeah, you want a line?

America as an Empire is on a down-hill trajectory. Don't ask me to calculate that using physics equations. Ask some Chinese guy at MIT to do that. You know that these Chinese like that shit. But I am American, and I just like to chill and flip on the TV and forget about physics. There's no application in life, and that means, it's unnecessary. These Chinese can't speak no English, but they can do physics. God, I hope that they are not building weapons to target America. Looking at those Chinese people at MIT, I say America stands no chance. And to make it worse. People in the American command center are probably doing a line of cocaine, regulasrly, so they'll miss everything.

In China, I have heard that they kill you if they find like an ounce of cocaine on your body. Or is it Singapore? It's one of those Chinese looking countries with Chinese sounding languages. No wonder they can do so good physics! After lines and lines of cocaine, brain don't work so good. It's like, it's like, a little bit, slower. You know what I mean? Slower. And those literature discussions don't require quick thinking, and you can bullshit through it. You can't do that with physics. There is actually a correct answer.

Americans do not understand the concept of growing up. Hey, I am not complaining. I am an American, after all. But look at Las Vegas. What the heck is that? Toyland for adults. They have like mini-me buildings for everything. Venice. Eiffel Tower. New York. Geez! It's like Disneyland syndrome. Since it's a bit awkward going to Disneyland if you don't have any kids, you go to Las Vegas. They have some amusement rides that accommodate your middle-aged back and hips. How much jiggling do you think a middle-aged body will take? Disneyland could put some middle-aged American in a coma. Las Vegas is slower, accommodates your obese body with all-you-can-eat buffet, and makes you feel good about yourself with a 2 minute walk around the mini-Venice place. Yeah, you can live in denial and feel like a child without being pointed out as a retard for doing "children" things. That's the value of Las Vegas.

Is it any wonder that the Chinese and the Indians are beating the USA? If the Chinese and the Indians learn management, we Americans are screwed! Thankfully, Wharton and Harvard Business School are in the USA, and Asians are still suffering from colonialism and feel that psychological need to work for a white man that American companies can use software engineers from Bangalore like slaves at a fraction of their value and Chinese workers in Beijing to work for 1 dollar per day. But if the Indians and Chinese create their own Microsoft and Facebook, we are screwed!

Harvard and Wharton and Ivy League schools serve a purpose. Maybe God has not completely abandoned America, after all. But still, I hold to my thesis that God does not bless America. And I am a product of the cursed generation in America facing complete deterioration of the United States of America. Rise and fall of the American Empire. Dope will do that to you.

"No, I did not inhale." Yep, that about sums it up, alright, for the Bloomers. And Bloomers are the leaders of America of today. What does that mean? Doping through the day and doping through the policies. And thanks to the Bloomers, the later generations have inherited the doping tradition and culture. Line after line.

Although I am a part of this cursed generation in America which is roller-coastering toward Hell, I would like to find some kind of peace and comfort zone within it. After all, even in the fiercest wars and the most horrible period in history, people have managed to find solace and comfort. Peace exists in the midst of turmoil. And I am trying to find my peace as the American Empire quickly degenerates toward destruction.

America is playing bully in trying to sanction Syria, and America is finally realizing that they cannot play god among the nations. Russia and China no longer fear or respect America. And Russia and China are willing to stand up to America the bully.

Let's face it. Did we in America invade Iraq to give the Iraqi people better things in life? Maybe some may believe that. But this is how I see it. Bush junior had to save his dad's face, so he did it for dad. Bush senior had a lot of criticism for not "finishing his job" in Iraq, and Bush junior, who loves his dad, thought he was saving his dad's honor. Hey, can't blame the son for wanting to save his dad's honor!

Why did the US military do it? Well, they wanted to try out their sophisticated weapons. When else can you test the advanced weapons on real people, except during a war? Shooting at cardboard can be fun at times, but it's certainly at a different level of entertainment than shooting a moving target. Thinking target? Well, you have read Edgar Allen Poe's short story. That's the Greatest Game!

Why did the American people go along with it? Well, 9-11 hurt American pride. Bunch of camel-humping Arabs took down our two tall buildings in New York. Heck, no camel-humping Arabs are going to get away with it. Since we don't know which camel-humping Arab did it, we'll just shoot the Hell out of the camel-humping Arabs we have excuse to shoot and kill. Candidate number one? Saddam Hussein. It was just

Saddam Hussein's bad luck that the American people were looking to kill some camel-humping Arabs.

Why is America trying to impose sanctions on Syria? Well, obviously, we have to look like we are still the Empire that tries to maintain control in the Empire, which covers the whole world. And that means putting local heads in his place. And Assad is one such local head, whose place he can be reminded of.

Unfortunately for the USA, China and Russia are standing up and not allowing America from exerting American sphere of influence.

How about the children? Is Syria really killing children and women in Syria? Maybe, so. But don't you think that we killed children and women when we bombarded Iraq with our bombs? Heck. If we count the number of Iraqis who died after we "saved" Iraq, that would make us Evil Killer Number One. China and Russia just see through our hypocrisy, and we just don't like it.

Really. What is a leader to do when there is massive rebellion? Just step down? That's what happened in America during mass revolts, right? Right. Assad is responding to massive insurrection, and he is just doing what any government would do against an armed rebellion. Can you really fault Assad for that? Really? Assad is doing exactly what American government or the American military would do if we had the same situation in America.

Yeah, I know the argument. We have free speech in America, so people won't do that. But suppose if people do? Have you heard of Branch Davidians? What we do in the USA is that if we think there is going to be a group of armed insurrectionists, we invade their home with SWAT team and kill half of them. We get them before they get to the Syria stage, where they are actually carrying out the armed rebellion.

What do you think the Patriot Act is doing? It is used mostly against Americans to monitor the domestic situation. You can be recorded right now, if you mention some insurrectionist words. Have you tried to open a bank account? You will see the Patriot Act sign, right in front of you. Yeah, you are being monitored, right now. And if there is even a small hint of armed organization, you can expect to see a whole SWAT team staring at you with their M-16 squeezed against your bleeding nose in your living room. That's why we can act high-and-mighty and act like we are holier-than-thou with Syria.

We Americans achieve peace by killing everyone off. We used that against Native Americans and we used that against the Japanese. That is the American way. But when we see others trying to imitate our technique? Well, that just can't be. Ain't no one going to go annihilating without our permission. Dang, nabit!

Russia and China were afraid to stand up to America in the past, but America ain't that powerful any more. So, they are standing up for what they perceive as American bullying tactics around the world. The world is a different place, now. China and Russia will not jump and play dead when we order it to. China and Russia ain't our bitch no more.

What does this mean? I dunno. History is exciting because anything can happen. Can Russia invade America and preemptively fire all of their nuclear missiles against America? Anything is possible. Can China invade America with advanced Navy? Anything is possible. That's what makes history interesting. Empires rise and fall. That much we know from history, so it won't be surprising if that happens to America.

Will it be surprising? Probably. Because when we see empires that fall, they seem surprised when it happens. Historical perspective is different from going through something. I guess that's the case life generally. When you break up with your girlfriend, it feels like the world is collapsing. But your parents are like, "You want syrup with that?" They treat the day like it's like any other day. Don't they know that the world has ended? Apparently, not. When you are going through it, it feels different. And as much as your parents love you, they will never understand your pain the way you understand your own pain.

When you get that rejection letter from Dartmouth College, you will cry because it is so painful, and you had worked so hard for it and had given up so much for it. And your mom may cry because she sees tear marks in your face. Your dad may just say, "Don't act like a girl, you big wuss!" Or, you may have a sensitive dad who may shed a tear, too. But however many tears your parents will shed for your rejection letter from Dartmouth College, they will never ever know how it feels, because they are not you. They did not give up all those things that you gave up for Dartmouth. You gave them up. So, when you are rejected, you are hit particularly hard. Your mind subconsciously processes everything that you gave up for Dartmouth and adds exponential value to your pain. Your pain is four-dimensional and involves time. Years and years you had sacrificed for Dartmouth. Your parents cannot begin to understand or feel that pain. No one can. Only you can feel that pain.

In the same way, there is no way others will understand what it means and how it feels when the American Empire falls, as Americans do. This sentiment can be likened to the Olympic games. When India loses a gold metal to Pakistan by a fraction of one second, no one can feel that pain the way Indians do. And no one can feel the jubilation that the Pakistanis feel, the way that Pakistanis feel it, if you are not Pakistani. There is a shared experience and shared identity.

In the same way, when the American Empire falls, Americans will feel collective pain, that no others will feel. And the new Empire that rises will feel jubilation, and no one outside of that group can really feel that jubilation. I guess it is not unlike the Super Bowl. When two teams play against each other, the cities behind the teams are attached to the teams.

Thus, if New York Giants play against New England Patriots, you could probably hear a collective celebration in New York City when Giants score a touchdown, and at the same time, you will hear a collective yelping of pain in the city of Boston. The identity that New Yorkers feel for the Giants will actually cause them happiness when their football team receives a touchdown, and Bostonians will feel the pain that others cannot comprehend. Super Bowl is not just a game, it is an experience for the two cities. It can be described as a tale of two cities. It was the best of times, and it was the worst of times. It is the best times, because their team is playing in the Super Bowl. It is the worst of times, because economy is doing so badly. The housing market is down, and both New Yorkers and Bostonians who own property have lost a lot of money with the downturn of the economy. Some may have lost their jobs. Most have lost value in their IRA or other types of retirement savings. It is absolutely the worst of times that they never imagined would happen to them.

And because it is the worst of times that the Super Bowl 2012 feels so important for New Yorkers and Bostonians. They need something to give them that positive push, and the Super Bowl win can be that positive push. Just like someone who has nothing to live for is willing to die for his country, just like a selfish person is willing to die for his girlfriend and her love, no matter how foolish it looks to those on the outside, the 2012 Super Bowl between New York and Boston is not just about a game. It is about hope. It is about identity. It is about future.

At a time like this, saying the wrong word can get you shot or stabbed. People are willing to kill for their football team and die for their football team. The sentiment can be identified with a Marine who thinks that he is doing the right thing, killing women and children during the Vietnam War. Those damn Gook Communists. Die, Gooks! Die, Communists! Die, All!

The build-up to the Super Bowl is like no other time, because it is the best of times, and it is the worst of times.

Mostly, it is the worst of times. If it is on an election year, there is lot more riding on it. A Patriot Win would give Mitt Romney, the former Massachusetts governor, the push that he thinks will help clench his Republican victory. And Romney would milk all that he can. All the other candidates are just hoping that the Patriots will lose, because they are thinking that a Patriot defeat may be seen as bad luck for Romney by the nation that will be glued to the TV on Super Bowl Sunday. It's not just a game. It is a gladiatorial contest for life and death. Mitt Romney's political life or death.

People can be very superstitious, and people are always looking for a sign. The gladiatorial contest between the Patriots and the Giants is a contest with national significance in an election year. If the Patriots win, Mitt Romney will milk it for everything its worth to win the Presidency. If the Patriots lose, then the other candidates will milk it to wage psychological war on Mitt Romney and his camp. And this psychological assault will be effective because the devastation from the football defeat is like your gladiator being killed by the gladiator from the other side.

It's like the fight between David and Goliath. There is one fighter representing a nation fighting a fighter from another nation. The victory of the gladiator signifies the victory of the nation. When David defeated Goliath, the Philistines were so demoralized that Israel won the war. Of course, the Philistines could have defeated Israel. The Philistines were mightier and better equipped and better trained than the Israelites. There is a reason why on one wanted to stand against Goliath. Everyone in Israel expected defeat, even before the war began. The side that should have won lost simply because the mightiest gladiator was killed. One man can change history. One man can change the outcome of what people thought to be a done-deal by the both sides. The Super Bowl, which is out of the hands of Mitt Romney, is such a contest. The Patriot defeat can singlehandedly defeat Mitt Romney, if his opponents exploit it.

Obviously, Mitt Romney is like the Philistines and the others are like David.

The significance of gladiatorial contest can be seen as valued in the Bible as well. In the Book of Isaiah 6:8, God says, "Whom should I send? Who will go for us?" And Isaiah responds and says, "Here I am! Send me!" This shows that God of the Bible operates along gladiatorial lines, and Isaiah was the one gladiator who represented God. Single-man theory is very strong in the Bible. Abraham being the father of the nations. Jesus Christ being the only Savior of the World. One-man theory of history operates in the Bible and even in secular history of the west.

Achilles versus Hector in combat in Troy represents the kind of gladiatorial contest with consequence that matches the gladiatorial contest between David and Goliath. And the contest between the Patriots and the Giants represents a gladiatorial contest between Mitt Romney's Representative, the Patriots, and the Giants, the gladiator fighting for the rest of the Republican pack, whom the media has written off. A win by Patriots is a win for Romney, whether the Patriots like it or not. That's just the way the cookie crumbles at this point in history.

It's like when the Atom Bomb was dropped on Hiroshima and Nagasaki, the soldiers were just following orders. They did not sign up to carry out genocide or desire it necessarily. It's like the SS of the Nazis. When they achieved being the elite unit of the Nazi military machine, many men in the elite SS did not sign up for annihilation of the Jews, but the cookie crumbled that way, because of the flow of history.

Achilles did not ask to be born to fight for the Greeks, and Hector was just born that way. Lady Gaga could crone until she becomes coarse, but her song speaks one truth. Robert E. Lee fought for the South not because he believed in the right to slavery, but because he was a Southerner and he wanted to fight on the side of his family and friends to protect their life. Wars are like that. Gladiatorial contest is like that.

And that is why the Patriots represent Romney and the Giants are against Romney. Enemy of your enemy is your friend. The Super Bowl, like the Gladiatorial Contests of the Roman Empire, is fraught with significance and historical ramifications. Some historians say that the Olympic Games in Germany over which Hitler presided as the Chancellor of Germany sealed his plan for World War 2 and gave Germans their sense of destiny of the Third Reich. Economic historians say that the Olympic Games in Seoul is what elevated Samsung, LG, and Hyundai into international powerhouses. Political historians say that the Olympic Games in Beijing broke down the political mental blocks in the world to give China its Free Trade status that had the domino effect of destroying Japan's economic edge and making Japan economically unnecessary in the world and starting the demise of the American Empire. Now, many predict the future downfall of the United States of America as the dominant global power. Some say that the 2012 Olympics in London will be the make-it-or-break-it event for the European Union and Europe's economic future, so the United Kingdom is paranoid about terrorist attacks and every terrorist in the planet is trying to initiate a terrorist attack, however small, in London during Olympic Games, because it would be a symbolic act that would match any catastrophic event, such as 9/11 or even out-do it.

Gladiatorial contests are significant and can change the course of history. Olympic Games matter more than how historians calculate. A smart politician would learn to exploit the Super Bowl to his advantage, because it can change the odds the way David's victory changed the odds for the Israelites. Sometimes, games and sports events matter more than thousands of ads, millions of political commentaries, and zillions of endorsements. The Roman Empire understood the significance of the Gladiatorial Contests, and so did the Greeks. Apparently, the Israelites did not, although the Philistines did, but fortunately for the Israelites, they "accidentally" benefitted from the gladiatorial contest, which is a kind of sporting event.

The Super Bowl 2012 can change not only the US Republican Primaries, but it can determine the outcome of the US Presidential Elections. Not only that, the Super Bowl 2012 can jump start the economy in ways that all the stimulus packages have failed to do in relative terms. Even beyond that, the Super Bowl 2012 can change the course of history in the internet connected age, when all of the world can access the game, even in the poorest areas of the world, like Bangladesh and tribal regions of Africa.

Sports move people in ways that literature cannot, because literature is inaccessible for the illiterate and the uneducated. Sports is accessible to all, and more importantly, it is entertaining even for the educated, so it can even impact the literati in the most elite societies. There is a reason why sports players are paid more than college professors. It's explainable by the simple capitalist principle of supply and demand. There is demand across party-lines, education levels, socio-economic classes, and political ideologies. And that is why major sporting events can shift history.

It is no accident that the Bible uses sporting terminology and the ideas of sports that were current at that time. People can relate to major sporting events. Of course, opportunity does not always mean profit for all. Sporting events can come and go and may not help someone because he does not know how to utilize it, even though at times, it can "accidentally" help, like in the case of David. Although David did not understand the significance fully, the perceived significance of the event by the Philistines contributed to the outcome of victory for the Israelites when there was no chance of Israelites winning. So, even if one side does not put value into a major sporting event, the side that puts value to the sporting event will read into the outcome of the sporting event.

Just because a little boy kills a big gladiator does not mean that Israelites now have a better chance of winning. Just because David won by beginners' luck does not mean that the Israeli army suddenly became a better trained army or a better equipped army. But that reality was irrelevant to the Philistines and the Philistine military personnel. The Super Bowl 2012 must be seen in the same light. It is significant beyond what is visible, and it exerts power, which is very real in a sense, in ways that cannot be fully comprehended. Obviously, it will take historians 50 years or more from now to unpack the significance and impact of Super Bowl 2012. Historians will argue over finer points. But one thing is unmistakable. Super Bowl 2012 may be the most significant event that impacts 2012 US Presidential Elections than all the political debates and newspaper articles and TV ads combined.

History is interesting because one man, David, can change the course of history. History is significant because of the potential of one football team to change the course of American history and through that the course of world history. Which team wins or loses at Super Bowl 2012 is not just about a game, it can mean the rise and fall of nations, the rise and fall of political figures, and the future course of the world economy. Whether the players or the viewers understand the intangible power of the event is irrelevant, and that is what makes history interesting.

Marketers understand the relevance from economic standpoint a little bit, because 30 second ad in the Super Bowl can run millions of dollars. There is obviously a reason why companies are willing to spend that kind of money for thirty seconds. There is a reason why Madonna is performing at half-time, because the Baby Boomers, who by in large rule America, now, in every sector, grew up idolizing her music, much in the same way that the modern teenage generation grows up idolizing Lady Gaga. But the current generation of teenagers will not have power for at least 20 years, and a lot can happen from now until then.

What may be interesting is to see which politicians effectively utilize the event to their advantage. Obviously, that can only be analyzed effectively in hindsight by historians 50 years from, now. Current Lady Gaga generation will be the ones analyzing it. And it would be fun to read their analysis, if I am still alive, then.

Chapter 4

I can't believe that I am still on this bus. I don't think I have been on the bus for so long. In the USA, we rarely take the bus. Actually, I guess I should speak for myself. I remember talking with a buddy of mine in college, and he said that he knew someone who took the bus from San Antonio, Texas, all the way to Philadelphia to attend his son's graduation from the University of Pennsylvania. I wonder how poor they are. I have never heard of anyone doing that, except for criminals who just finished their jail time.

How many days of bus ride is that? I think he said that it was something like 3 days on the bus, including overnight buses and sleeping at bus terminals. Geez. This man was supposed to be a Southern Baptist preacher. How much do Southern Baptist preachers make any way? You would figure that they should have enough money to fly to the son's college graduation. I have heard that Southern Baptists are mostly poor, trailer folk, who work for minimum wage at Stop-and-Shop or doing odd jobs in the neighborhood. They are good, honest folk, who work hard for their money and take pride in their work. Protestant work ethic, some would say. But Southern Baptists tend to be poor, nonetheless. I guess all the work does not enrich them. It's hard to become rich, unless one went to an exclusive college in the East Coast. I guess that's true for Texas as well. From what I hear, most Southern Baptists start working right out of high school or go to a state university. So, many of them fail to have top level jobs. But three days of bus ride. That is brutal.

But you have to recognize one thing. America is a really generous country. My friend said that the University of Pennsylvania gave him so much scholarship that he was able to pay for two roundtrip tickets back home without any problem. In fact, the scholarship that he received included not only full-tuition scholarship, but it also included full scholarship for dormitory costs, full scholarships for 20 meals per week at PENN's dining hall, where each meal is over 10 dollars. And the scholarship also gave him several hundred dollars to buy new clothing, and books for his courses, and other "incidental things" like night out on weekends with friends to see a musical or a movie. I guess studying hard in high school really pays off, especially for poor people like him. His father takes 3 days of buses – that's 72 hours of straight bus-riding and bus-terminal-staying to get to his son's college graduation, but the son flies back home two times per year at PENN's expense and lives like any other PENN student. PENN must have paid over $260,000 on him. That's a quarter million dollars! That's a price of a really nice house in Pennsylvania. I don't think there is any other country in the world, where smart students can get a break like that. No wonder why everybody is trying to come to America. If parents are smart and encourage their children, then three children going to the University of Pennsylvania means getting $750,000 free. What a country!

I can identify with the pain of the bus-riding, although I cannot really say that it is pain because I am sitting next to a very attractive woman who looks more and more attractive with every second. Isn't it kind of strange how a woman becomes more beautiful as you spend more time with her? It's a strange thing. Hadas is not unattractive, but she is no Miss Israel, either, if you were to look at it from an objective standpoint. But I guess beauty is really in the eyes of the beholder.

Since I have all this time on the bus, I guess I can indulge myself and reflect on my past experiences. It is interesting, because I never get to do that in the USA. I am always on one electric device or another, and it's so go-go-go, all the time. But in this long, and I mean long, bus ride, with a partner who is apparently getting her dose of beauty sleep, there is the luxury to think back and reflect. By the way, how many hours can she sleep like that? Although she does look cute in a cuddly sweepy-baby kinda way.

I remember a girlfriend that I had, and I swear to God that I experienced something that was so weird, biologically. It's like, "My eyes are deceiving me, dude, and I ain't on anything. Maybe the government put stuff in the air." Yep, it was strange, because an ugly woman transformed herself before my very eyes into the most beautiful woman in the world. And I went from, "Geez, she's ugly," to "I miss you so much," after not seeing her for a few hours. And that was the strangest thing.

I remember seeing her for the first time. I said to myself, "God, she's ugly. I mean she is fuckin' fugly!" Obviously, I tried to keep my thoughts to myself in my mind and not give away my thoughts. But I was never good at the Poker Face thing, so I think I might have shown her my repulsion. It's bad, because I am generally a nice guy. I try to be nice to everyone. So, I tried to be nice to her. But maybe because of her lack of pulchritude, I found myself being irritated with things she said. So, more than a few times, I corrected her in a rude way. And I was really mean about it. "Don't be so stupid." I don't know why I was so cruel. But maybe they are right when they say an ugly woman makes men mean. I was being mean to her without knowing why.

But it was strange, because it seemed to fascinate her. Maybe she has not been treated in a mean way before. After all, her father was a multimillionaire executive of some Fortune 500 company. Couldn't she get some plastic surgery or something with all that money? My friend explained to me after the fact that she was too young at the age of 17 to get plastic surgery because she had not fully developed, yet.

I could see some point. She was not really developed. She had a flat chest. You kinda felt like saying, "Where's the beef?" But of course, you didn't, because that just wouldn't be prudent. Gotta hand it to George. He said something that just sticks in your mind and prevents you from doing some stupid things. Thanks George!

But her chest was really flat. I can say that with 100% certainty because I actually got to handle them at length and for protracted length of time and viewed it from all different angels. I know it might sound crass, but I think I am a breast kind of guy, so I could never get bored with her breasts, even though they were flat. And they were so flat. You kind of put your hand over her breast, and the whole breast was covered. And she had a very tiny nipple to match her very tiny breasts. I mean, everything was flat.

Once I had a chance to view her breast though the hole in her tank top as she was bending. She wasn't wearing a bra for some reason. Maybe she was feeling hot. Or maybe she was trying to entice me to touch her breasts, which obviously, I did. They were so small that if they were on a man, I bet you would not feel that they were strange. That's how flat they were. I mean flat like the plains Indians territory flat. I mean like your school desk flat which you stare at when your biology teacher talks about sexual organs, and he has a strange grin on his face. I mean flat like waters in the lake on a hot summer day when nobody is taking a swim in the water because everyone is outside staring at the bare breasted blonde naturalist who is obviously breaking the laws of the state with her naturalism. Yep, they were really flat.

But the strange thing was that they satisfied me. And that was the strangest thing in the world. How could such breasts satisfy me? Well, I think it had to do with the fact that she seemed so happy under my hands covering her breasts. The look of true contentment on a woman as you touch her private organs is a sublime experience. I am not necessarily talking about pleasure. Of course, I hope that she felt pleasure and lots of it. But I did not notice that. What I saw was a look of contentment, a kind of deep happiness.

I remember her talking about us getting married. She warned me, "You have to do exactly as I say when you meet my dad, okay?" I looked at her in bewilderment. She was already talking about marriage, and I had known her only a few weeks. "My father wants me to marry someone like him, and so you have to act in a certain way." Geez. Was she for real? Apparently, she was. "He would have a problem with someone like you as his son-in-law." Yep, she had 2nd degree black belt in humiliating her boyfriend during intimate moments, and she was working on her 3rd degree black belt on how to make a grown man cry through humiliation.

Of course, I was so focused on her perky, albeit small, breasts that I just nodded and said, "Okay." But I think she was serious, because she had this "I am very serious" look in her face. And from that moment on, she frequently talked about us getting married.

I wondered why she did this. Maybe she was really in love. Maybe she had a Puritanical upbringing, and she could not fathom being fondled by a man who was not her husband apart from relating to him as her future husband. I did not know what her reasons were, but I was growing into the idea of marrying her. I enjoyed being with her, lying next to her, and touching her bare breasts. And I enjoyed playing with her hair. She did not ever complain, even though my touching her hair completely redirected the orientation of her hair. She would smile with a smile that broke her face, which looked so beautiful to me by then. I remember walking with her down to the pier and taking photos of her. I felt so proud to be next to her, holding her hand. And I felt that she was the most beautiful woman in the world. And I took many, many photos of her. And I tried to capture her face with sunlight hitting her in a peculiar way. Picture of her with the waves rolling behind her. Her with the background of the ship. Her with onlookers looking at her. I had completely forgotten that I had originally thought that she was the ugliest girl in the world when I first saw her. How strange that she had transformed herself so radically before my very own eyes.

I had often wondered why such a good looking guy was with such an ugly girl, when I chanced upon such a combination in the street or in the classroom. What did he see in her? And here I was, being that very weird guy, who was fawning over an ugly girl. Sometimes, I would wake up from my fantasy and remember that my first impression was that she was very ugly. And I tried to get proof. I opened my eyes wide and tried to see her ugliness. And I couldn't. That was strange, because somehow, I wasn't seeing what I was supposed to see. Obviously, she had not physically altered in last couple of weeks. Maybe she was a witch and she put a spell on me. No, upon longer thought, I don't think she's a witch, because her father was an elder in a big Presbyterian church, and she said that she was Christian.

Okay, I have to confess that some of the things that we were doing were not very Christian, and I felt guilty about it. But sometimes, not much, because I guess my sinful nature had taken over, and I was enjoying her naked body, too much. I guess St. Augustine could relate, because he used to be a player and had an illegitimate child before he was converted and became a saint. There is something sublime about a naked woman's body. And I guess those artists of the Renaissance understood that.

How was my vision transformed? Maybe it was the love of a good woman. She was a good woman, and there is no doubt about that. I guess I find that rich women tend to be good and kind. I don't know what it is. Maybe having plenty makes them more generously inclined so that their heart is kinder. Poor women have to fight to survive and their heart may become hard and unloving. This may not be the case, but I remember that every rich woman that I dated had a really good heart, even the bitchy ones. They were pussy cats underneath all the flash and pretention. They were actually vulnerable, nice women. And this ugly duckling turned beautiful swan girlfriend of mine also had a really nice heart.

I remember her taking me to a really nice restaurant. I was a flat broke college student, and she would pay for everything, including the tip and the cab fare. I did not have a dollar to my name, most of the time. And she did it so naturally, like I was a part of her family. I never felt inferior or that she was trying to be superior. I felt like it was natural, because she made it so natural.

Maybe it was the fact that she loved me so wholeheartedly that I fell in love without knowing. The moment we were in a relationship, she made me feel like I belonged. She made me feel that I belonged to her. The feeling of belonging, of being owned emotionally, made me feel a sense of connectedness with her. And she talked about us getting married like it was the most natural thing in the world. I believed in her dream, as she believed in her dream. And it became our dream. Not thinking about logistics or the current situation of my being in college, we talked together about being married, like it was going to happen in the next couple of months.

I knew she loved me, and I had no doubt. And that sense of emotional security allowed me to make myself vulnerable and give myself completely to her. I found myself longing for her.

For her presence. Just to be near her. And it became a dependency. I felt I needed her.

I remember her telling me one time, "I am going to see some movies." I said, "I'll come, too." She said, "You have tests tomorrow, so you should study. I will be okay." And she went to the movie and saw three movies.

After she had left for her country, I wondered if I was suffocating her or smothering her. She had never said that or even hinted that. But maybe that was what I was doing and she needed some time off. But I ached the whole night knowing that she was away, and I did not get much studying done. I was obviously in love and crazy about her.

I remember when she first made the gesture of affection, I was completely mortified. When I was walking in the street talking with her, she grabbed my arm, apparently in a sign of affection. I was mortified that an ugly girl was grabbing my arm. I was afraid about what my friends would say. I was afraid that people would say, "Did you hear? He is going out with that ugly girl." So, I brushed her arm aside. But she did not quit. She kept grabbing my arm. Four or five times, we went through this ritual. I felt so humiliated and embarrassed. And after that night, I just tried to ignore her.

What made it more angering was that she had latched herself with her friend, whom I was interested in. She was this beautiful Chinese girl who was studying at Stanford University, a university that I really liked. I could say, "My girlfriend goes to Stanford!" It satisfies my vanity, and I could brag about that. That alone would make me an alpha male among my male friends. But that was not all. This Chinese girl was a goddess. I kid you not. She is the most beautiful Asian girl that I saw in my life. And even today, I haven't met any Asian who looks as good as her.

When I first saw her, I could not feel my feet, because she was so beautiful. She ran track for Stanford, so you could imagine her body. She must have been 105 pounds and about

5'10". Her legs were pieces of art. You could just stare at the smooth, toned form of her beautiful legs for hours, if she let you. You would have been just content to look, because it looked so good. You did not even need to touch it. You would be like, "Thank you God for creating such beautiful legs and giving me the eyes to be able to appreciate your beautiful creation."

But her legs were not her best feature. You should have seen her face. My God! Her face was a face of an angel. Her smile made your heart jump a beat, every time she smiled. I could imagine someone having a heart attack just looking at her smiles. And her eyes twinkled like the stars in heaven as she looked at you, and you just could drink in her beauty and revel in it. She made you feel like somebody just because she was looking at you. And this was the girl that I was crazy about, and this is the girl that I desired. Not the ugly one.

And that night, I was going to make my move, come heaven or come hell. I could not stand it that I could be so close to an angel and not try to be with her. And I did not mind losing it all, just for one try. One try to have her. So, I arranged for this night. And who showed up? The ugly one. I was trying to be polite. I think that the beautiful Stanford girl brought her because she was absolutely not a competition. The ugly girl was not even pretty enough to be her slave. That was what I was thinking that night. I was talking to the ugly one, just because the angel had brought her. I wanted to impress the angel and show her that I had a nice heart. I talked with the ugly one, just to increase my chance with the angel.

But what happened? The ugly one kept groping at me. So, you could imagine how infuriated I was. She was messing up my chances with her, the perfect woman. I would be content just kissing the feet of that Stanford girl. She was so amazingly hot that I was certain that I would never again see someone like that. And I haven't to this day. I wonder where she is now.

But as you can see, the ugly girl so thoroughly sabotaged my chances that crucial night. And interestingly enough, the Stanford girl liked me, too. I still don't believe it, but apparently she did. How could she? Is she the heavenly being capable of loving a mortal like me? That's just not possible!

But what is stranger than that is that once I went out with the ugly duckling turned beautiful swan, I did not care at all. I think that the Stanford girl was upset that I ended up being coupled with her "friend." I remember her wanting to take revenge, so she walked right in front of me with some Adonis looking guy to a shower and taking shower together, just to make me suffer. They had common bathrooms for men and women at the dorm.

Strangely, I did not care, because I was in love with her. I only wanted her and was satisfied with her. It was strange to experience because I had previously wanted the Stanford girl so much and had intensely lusted after her perfect body. And she was not having any effect on me because I fell in love with the one whom I had originally thought was the ugliest girl in the world.

Even today, I regret not marrying her, even as I remember my first impression about her being so ugly. Even with years passed, I still think that it would have been the best decision of my life in terms of personal happiness. Even after having dated women who look like models, I think that she would have made me the happiest. I was so truly in love with her, and she was so much in love with me. I don't know if I will ever have that combination, again.

Some might say that we were too young to marry, but I would say that they were wrong. If you know you are madly and completely in love, then you should get married and share the rest of your life together. You can tell yourself that you will find another love like that, but probably you would be wrong. No, you won't find someone that you love to the same extent. And certainly you won't find a combination that you are absolutely certain of, which is that both of you love each other so completely.

I know one thing for sure. When I have kids in the future, and if they fall in love in high school, completely, so that they want to get married, I would not stop them. In fact, I would encourage them. I think anyone above 16 can get married and have happiness. Not marrying your high school sweetheart that you love is basically damning yourself to a lifetime of unhappiness. America was a happier country when high school sweethearts married each other. As people get older, love becomes more cynical and mechanical. People are always trying to find ulterior motives and expediencies. That is why when parents get involved in their children's love, they often ruin it, because parents inject adult cynicism to something that is pure, innocent, and beautiful. It is like adults thinking that Santa Claus is ridiculous.

I remember that on Christmas Eve, I would stay up as late as possible to meet Santa Claus. I thought he was real, and I wanted to see him and say, "Merry Christmas!" But no matter how late I stayed up at night, the Santa Claus did not show. When I fell asleep, the moment that I woke up, I saw a Christmas gift besides me. And I was so upset that I missed Santa Claus. Mom would say that next year might be the year that I get to see Santa, and I waited for the next year. But it was the same the next year. But I kept the hope alive, until some day, I stopped believing in Santa, and our family just exchanged gifts under the Christmas tree. Obviously, I found out that dad was Santa. But I am grateful to mom and dad that they did not tell me that, and that I found out about it with passing years. There was something very precious in my childhood.

The idea that people cannot do things if they are married is plainly wrong. I think being married young is a good thing because two people in love can encourage each other. They can be best friends, lovers, and constant companions. They would be much more productive because so many people waste time and energy due to loneliness or trying to find things to do to forget loneliness. Being married with someone you innocently love and wholeheartedly love would anchor you to be more stable. And with this stability, you have a greater chance of success. Ruth Bader had children during her Law School, and she is the Supreme Court Justice. The majority of the people who win Nobel Prize are married with children. Stability brings productivity. Insecurity brings loss of time and loss of opportunity.

This though is making me depressed, so I think I will be taking a nap. All I see is the desert outside and the extreme heat sending out heat waves. I could see Hadas next to me dreaming about something nice and sweet. She looks serene. I know my sleep will bring about such a serenity. If I could just fall asleep....

Chapter 5

I know I am asleep, because I am dreaming about something. I know that the dream cannot be real, because I am at Dartmouth College in my dream, and I have never been to New Hampshire in my life.

In my dream, I am in Dartmouth College and it looks strangely like my college. And in my dream, I am arguing with someone about something, but I cannot make out what I am arguing about. I don't really know why I am dreaming about Dartmouth College, and it makes me feel irritated, even in my dream. It's like dream imposing itself on me. Dartmouth College. What's at Dartmouth College?

After a long struggle at Dartmouth College, I wake up. Hadas is awake and looking at me.

"What's wrong?" Hadas looked with concern in her eyes.

"Nothing," I said, feeling the dryness of my throat. I take some sips of water.

"You look like you had a nightmare," Hadas does not give up.

"Really?" I said, surprised. "I did not really have a nightmare."

I can still see Hadas staring at me.

"But I did have a disturbing thought before I fell asleep," I said.

"What's that?" Hadas said.

"Well," I fished for ways to phrase the question. "Did you ever have a time when you thought someone was ugly and then he started to look good?"

Hadas looked at me. "You are not talking about me, are you?"

She looked a bit scared.

"No," I said, "Of course, not. You are attractive!"

"I know," Hadas said, playfully. "It's like me with you. I thought you were ugly when I first saw you, but now, you absolutely look gorgeous."

"Hey, hey, hey," I said, "I am not a girly boy. Don't call me gorgeous, or I might have to call the Palestinian special forces on you."

"I am an Israeli," Hadas said, "Not a Palestinian."

"Precisely!" I said and laughed.

Hadas caught the joke and laughed along.

"But seriously, did you have that happen?" I asked.

Hadas said, "No. Never."

Gee, thanks! Now, I feel like an abnormal person. But I did not convert my thoughts into speech. I said, "I guess most people don't."

"That's right. Nah-Hone!" Hadas said.

I was silent for a second. And I wanted desperately to change the subject.

"So, what places do you want to visit in Egypt?" I asked.

"Do you know what I really want to see?" Hadas asked.

"What is this? A Talmud class. Question with a question?" I joked.

"What? Telling an anti-semitic joke?" Hadas joked back.

"After all, we are going to an anti-semitic territory," I joked back. "When in Rome, do as the Romans do."

"When in Egypt, do as Egyptians do?" Hadas retorted.

94

"Of course," I said.

"Well, then," Hadas said, "You won't be getting some."

"What do you mean?" I said, surprised by her response.

"You know that the Egyptians are Muslims and they don't want unmarried people don't have sex," Hadas said.

I looked at her a bit surprised, because she looked serious. I said, "You look serious."

At these words, Hadas softened a bit. "I am just kidding, of course."

I said, "Does this mean that I will be getting some?"

Hadas hit me in the arm.

"It hurts! Your Israeli Defense Forces training has made you into a soldier so your fist is a lethal weapon. Be careful where you wave that thing."

"I could say the same thing for you," Hadas said, smiling.

"But I carry no weapons," I said. "I am a man of peace."

"You look innocent, but you are really dangerous, you know that?" Hadas said.

"Me? Dangerous?" I responded. "Nah."

We both laughed.

"So, what do you want to do in Egypt?" I revisited the topic.

"Well, one thing I like to see is Egyptians protesting," Hadas said.

"It's your Jewish side," I said. "You can't wait to see Arabs suffering."

"Will you lay off with my Jewish side!" Hadas said, somewhat seriously.

"Did you say, "Will you lay with my Jewish side?" If that's what you said, I would of course say, 'Yes, Ma'am!' " I said.

"Hey, cowboy," Hadas laughed. "Take a cold shower."

"Only if you will take it with me," I said.

"You are incorrigible," Hadas said.

"That is only because I have been bewitched by your beauty," I said.

"You are such a charmer," Hadas said.

"No, I am just a poor boy," I said, and then started to sing the song from Queens. "No, he's just a poor boy."

Hadas sang along.

We suddenly noticed Egyptian eyes glaring at us.

"Maybe it's sacrilege or something to sing Queen songs in Egypt," I said.

"You know they hate the west," Hadas said.

"Hey, hey, hey," I said, "Remember, we are not in Kansas anymore, and we have to follow the yellow brick road."

"Is that like an American attempt at allusion?"

"Yep," I said, "Name that movie!"

"I don't know the title of that movie!" Hadas said.

"Ah, Grasshopper," I said, trying to imitate the wise monk in the *Kung Fu* TV series, "You have so much to learn."

"Will you teach me?" Hadas said, smiling.

"I will teach you from head to toe," I said.

"Ah, so!" Hadas said and made an artificial buck teeth expression.

"Hadas, you are such a racist!" I said, smiling.

"No, I am not," Hadas said.

"Look at yourself in the mirror, Hadas," I said. "You are squinting your eyes and making buck teeth and you are saying, 'Ah, so!' That in my book would qualify you to be a bona fide racist."

"You are so serious!" Hadas. "It's just a joke."

"Talk to the hand," I said, putting my hand against her face.

"Hey, get off," Hadas said. "Your hand is so hot."

"You are so sweaty!" Hadas added.

"Oh, I see," I said. "You were thinking about me."

"Yeah, flatter yourself, Mr. Self-Flatterer," Hadas said.

"Now, I understand why you had that big smile on your face when you were sleeping," I said. "You were dreaming about me!"

"Yeah, keep dreaming, American boy," Hadas said.

"We may be dreaming for good, if we go see an Egyptian protest," I said.

"They can't be that dangerous," Hadas said.

"Are you kidding me?" I said. "The IDF has made you feel that you are bullet proof."

"Yeah, of course, I am bullet proof," Hadas said.

"Like that song?" I said, "Next time, I will be bullet proof?"

Hadas said, "Where did that line come from?"

"I don't remember, but the song goes, 'Next time, I will be bullet proof.' It's a pretty catchy tune, really."

"You know what's really catchy?" Hadas asked.

"What?"

"That song, 'Granade'!" Hadas answered.

"No, Hadas," I said. "That song is so stupid. I will grab a grenade for you, die for you, but you would not do the same? What kind of hell kind of stupid lyrics is that?"

"You have so much to learn about love," Hadas said.

Surprisingly, that comment hurt.

"And you have so much to learn about women," Hadas added.

"You may be right," I said. "Why don't you teach me a thing or too."

"Who's the cricket, now?" Hadas said.

"No, Grasshopper!" I said. "It's Grasshopper, not cricket!"

"Here's something," Hadas said. "Do you know that women like to talk at the date and want the guy to just add brief accompaniment comments?"

"No," I said, "I don't agree. I think women like it when guys tell funny jokes and say things to entertain."

"Yes, Mr. Penis," Hadas said, "Your Pennisness understands the women."

"Hey, hey, hey," I said, "Hold the sarcasm, please, or you won't get any tip."

"What's this with allusion to American culture!" Hadas said. "There is no tipping in Israel."

"Yeah, right," I said. "You are saying that if I leave a tip in Israel, the waitress will come running and say, "Sir, you forgot your money?"

"I thought you wanted to hold the sarcasm," Hadas said.

"You got me, there," I said.

"Okay, I will take the lesson number one with bitter pills," I said. "Let the woman talk in a date. Check!"

"How about lesson number two?" I said.

"Hey, eager-beaver American boy with intense work ethic and I-want-it-now fastfood demands," Hadas said, "Let's leave lesson number two for another day."

"It's like the James Bond movie title, 'Die Another Day,'" I said.

"My advice is not like dying," Hadas said.

"I know, but I feel like I am like James Bond," I said. "Like an American one."

"Hah!" Hadas said. "That's funny! You, a James Bond!"

"What's so funny about it?"

"James Bond is a real man," Hadas said.

"What the hell does that mean?" I responded. "And I am not?"

"No, you are a lovely little man," Hadas said.

"Little man?" I repeated in a frail voice.

"I mean that in the most positive way," Hadas said.

"How could being called a little man be a compliment?" I demanded, puzzled.

"It's like a term of endearment," Hadas said. "It's like saying, 'Sweetheart.'"

"I don't think 'little man' is the same as 'sweetheart,'" I said.

"Some guys like that," I said.

"Yes, Miss Vagina in her Supreme Vaginaness," I said. "You Viginaness knows everything about us men."

"Yes, Vagina must be worshipped as a god," Hadas said.

"Okay, you got a point there," I said. "Many men do."

"Precisely," Hadas said. "We are right because we are Goddess Vagina."

"Okay, you got a point there," I said.

"What are you? Keeping a point system?" Hadas said.

"But let's get to the major point, here," I said. "I am like James Bond, the American version. Notice the emphasis on the word, *American*. We Americans are not British. Ergo, I am not really like James Bond, the British agent. I am like the Secret Agent Man, American style."

"Oh, I see," Hadas said.

"But you know why I am like James Bond?" I asked.

"What?" Hadas humored me.

"Because I have a beautiful woman by my side," I said.

"Well, I agree with the beautiful woman part," Hadas said.

"That confirms my case," I said.

"But don't these beautiful women try to kill James Bond?" Hadas said.

"Yes, sometimes," I said, "But not all the time. Generally, the beautiful women sleep with James Bond."

"Are you making a pass at me, Mr. American James Bond?" Hadas said.

"Maybe," I said, laughing. "And what if I am? What would you say to that?"

Hadas looked at me with a twinkle in her eyes. She said," We'll just have to see, won't we? This movie is not yet finished."

"And this movie is like a James Bond movie, because there are exotic scenes in the background," I said.

"Talking about exotic, we will have to see the Giza Pyramids," Hadas said.

"Oh, that goes without saying," I said.

"They are so beautiful in the pictures," Hadas said.

"And they will look even more beautiful up close," I said.

"Oh, James, American James," Hadas said with fake emotion, "Do you really think so?" And she held my arm.

"Yes, my little woman," I said, playing along, "I know it will. I just know it will!" And I kissed her on the forehead.

"Oh, James, American James," Hadas said, "I just can't wait." And she rolled her eyes with a smile on her face. And we both cracked up laughing.

"So, we'll ride a horse around the Pyramids," I said.

"Can we ride on the Pyramids?" Hadas said.

"There you are, Temptress!" I said in a fake mocking voice. "Thy name is Eve."

"What did I say?" Hadas asked, puzzled.

"Ride ON," I said and paused for a second and winked at Hadas, "the Pyramids."

"Oh, I see we need to take you down to the Nile River and do some baptism to cleanse your mind, Mr. Fallen Adam," Hadas said.

"Whatever," I said and held up one hand. "Talk to the hand, girl!"

"You mean, 'my little woman'?" Hadas said.

"Whatever," I said again. "Talk to the hand! Mmm. Mmm. Mmm."

"You are so," Hadas said. "So...."

"I know," I said. "My awesomeness leaves you without words. This has been known to happen to a lot of women. That is why I am the American James Bond. You see?"

"I won't dignify that with a response, James, American James," Hadas said.

"Okie, dokie," I said. "Let's see what else we can see in Egypt."

"A protest," Hadas said, grabbing both of my hands with hers. "Oh, please, let's see a protest."

"What's in it for me?" I aked. Hadas looked at me, puzzled. "You are asking me to brave death and danger."

"But you are James, American James," Hadas said. "Danger is your middle name."

"Actually, McCord is my middle name," I said.

"McCord like McDonald's," Hadas said.

"I don't get it," I said.

"Who cares?" Hadas said. "It sounds provocative."

"Okay," I said, although I did not quite understand what she meant.

"Wow," Hadas said. "Now, I have two points! How many points do you have?"

"I must have at least a couple dozen," I said.

"Well," Hadas said. "You didn't call it, so you have zero points."

"But," I started to protest.

"Fair is fair," Hadas said.

"Not according Macbeths," I said. "Fair is foul."

"Huh?" Hadas responded.

"And foul is fair," I said.

"What's Macbeths?" Hadas said.

"Oh, you ignorant camel riding Middle Easterner," I mocked. "You don't know *Macbeth* by Shakespeare."

"Is he the same anti-Semite who wrote *The Merchant of Venice* and made Shylock the Jew look evil?"

"What's this with you and anti-semitism?" I asked.

"There are a lot of bad anti-semites in the world," Hadas said, half-serious.

"And there are lots of goblins and dwarfs and smurfs and fairy-god-mothers, too," I said.

"Now, you are mocking our religion," Hadas said.

"No, I am mocking your witch-hunting tone," I said. "Haven't you read, *The Crucible*? You create your own hell by creating fear and creating witches to hang."

"We are not doing that!"

I responded, "What 's this Shakespeare the Anti-Semite, then?"

"Okay, let's change the subject," Hadas said.

"One point!" I exclaimed.

"What?" Hadas said, surprised.

"I have a point. I called it!" I said and stuck my tongue out. "Nah, nah, nah, nah, nah." I teased Hadas.

"But you are still losing," Hadas said. "Two to one."

"Not for long, Buffy the Vampire Slayer!" I said.

"What's that?" Hadas said.

"Don't you watch American TV?" I asked.

"Of course, not," Hadas responded. "I am Israeli, so I watch Israeli TV."

"Honey, you don't know what you are missin'," I said and shook my head in fake mockery.

"Buffy the Vampire Slayer is a TV show about this girl who kills Vampires," I said.

"Sounds like fun," Hadas said. "Does she kill anti-semites, too?"

"You would like that, wouldn't you?" I said.

"Now, that's an American TV show that I would get Satellite TV to watch," Hadas said, half-serious.

"No, Buffy wears a cross," I said. "If you remember, Vampires are allergic to the cross and church items, like the holy water."

"So, the Vampires are the Jews?" Hadas said.

"I never thought of it like that before," I said. "But your Jewish perspective does shed some light on possible authorial intent."

"My Jewish perspective!" Hadas said. "Look at the way that you talk!"

"What?" I said. "Are you going to call me an anti-semite, too?"

"You may be influenced by the anti-semitism in your culture."

"And what culture is that?" I said.

"The Christian culture," Hadas said.

"Christian culture?" I asked.

"Christianity is anti-Semitic," Hadas said. "The New Testament makes Jews look evil and accuses the Jews of killing Jesus Christ, who is supposedly this great teacher."

"Actually, we Christians believe that Jesus Christ is God," I said.

"So, you think that Jews killed Jesus, too?" Hadas said.

"Well, I do believe in the New Testament," I said.

"Does that mean you hate Jews?" Hadas said.

"I don't hate you, Hadas," I said. "In fact, I am liking you, more and more, with each passing minute."

Hadas blushed.

"You, too, right?" I said.

"Don't flatter yourself!" Hadas said and punched me in the arm, again.

"Ouch!" I said. "Watch that IDF trained arm!"

"Sorry," Hadas said.

"Okay, so explain further," I said. "Buffy is a teenager and many guys had crush on her because she is attractive. She's married to Freddie Prinze, Jr."

"No!" Hadas said.

"You know Freddie?" I said.

"Yeah, he's so hot!" Hadas said.

"Not as hot as the other Freddie!" I joked.

"Who's the other Freddie?" Hadas asked.

"The other Freddie has longer fingers and they are solid as a rock, or steel, for that matter," I said and tried to keep a straight face. "And he wears this awesome sweater that matches this cool hat. And he has a permanent plastic-face for his face. And he's the kind of guy who shows up in your dreams and just rocks your world or turns your world upside down. His movies are big slashers."

"I don't know this term, 'slasher,'" Hadas said with curious eyes.

"Slasher means fun," I said with a managed straight face. "He's the cooler Freddie."

"Really?" Hadas said. "I have to see this Freddie?"

"We'll rent some DVD's when we get back to Israel, and you will have the night of your life. You will be screaming with delight or something else."

Hadas said, "Sounds like fun."

"Fun does not begin to describe it," I said and winked.

"I can't wait," Hadas said, getting interested.

"But for now, let's think Egypt," I said. "So, we know two things that we will do. One, the pyramids. Two, protests. Now, I have to get something out of this. Let me think." I paused for a second. "I know! You have to be like my Egyptian slave and give me a full body massage, as if I were a Egyptian Pharaoh himself."

"Do I have to?" Hadas said.

"Do you want to see the protests? Mayhem. Revolt. People screaming. Military crackdown. Possible danger to my life. I could lose my arm or something. Do you really want to go through that?"

"Okay," Hadas said. "I will be a slave for a day."

"That's even better. I was thinking more like 30 minutes, but I ain't going to complain," I said.

"30 minutes," Hadas said. "That's even better."

"Oh!" I exclaimed. "Me and my big mouth."

"Ha, ha!" Hadas mocked.

"Okay, 30 minutes," I said. "We have three things on the list, now."

"Massaging you isn't related to Egypt," Hadas said.

"For me, it is an Egyptian experience, because I will be roll-playing an Egyptian god-leader Pharaoh," I said, gleaming, "And it will be an Egyptian experience for you, too, my Egyptian slave."

"Okay," Hadas said, "Just rub it in."

"My little Egyptian slave," I said, "and I mean that in the most affectionate way."

"I bet you do!" Hadas feigned anger.

"Can I propose another thing?" I said, perhaps out of elation. I was psyched about the forthcoming massage by Hadas. "Let's take a ride down the Nile."

"Sounds like fun!" Hadas beamed with joy.

"Nile has been there for thousands of years," I said. "We can picture Moses floating down the Nile as a little baby inside a basket. And we can imagine Cleopatra and Mark Anthony riding down the Nile as illicit lovers." And I gave Hadas a wicked, come-hither look.

To my surprise, Hadas throw back an even more wicked, come-hiether look.

"A point for yo!," I said.

"What was that point for?" Hadas asked.

"I am just happy that you will give me an Egyptian Pharaoh massage," I said.

"Hey, I will take advantage of your disorientation," Hadas said. "After all, we learned about taking advantage of our enemies in the IDF. Three to one!"

"I knew it!" I said. "You are like the James Bond woman."

"I won't tell," Hadas said. "You will have to find out."

"Will you let me?" I said, playing along with her tease.

"That depends," Hadas said. "I myself do not know yet what I will choose. Will I raise my thumb up or put my thumb down."

"Nice, nice," I said. "An allusion to Rome."

"Well, it works especially fine, because you are a Christian," Hadas said.

"Oh, I see, just because I am a Christian, you want to throw me in the Pagan Roman amphitheater and play with your thumbs over my life and death," I said.

"Well," Hadas said with an evil gleam in her eyes, "Something like that, James Bond, American James Bond."

"I will get it where I can, as we Americans like to say," I said.

"What does that mean?"

"It's hard to explain, little lady," I said. She smiled. And there was a slight awkward moment.

"I propose that we also visit Thebes," I said to alter that uneasy atmosphere.

"Thebes, it is!" Hadas said. "The city of the kings."

"It's going to be the ultimate tourist experience," I said.

"You don't think that it will be dangerous?" Hadas asked.

"Hey, you are the one who actually want to see a protest, and what are you complaining about?" I chided.

Hadas was silent and looked down.

I said to appease her, "Besides, the Egyptian protests have nothing against tourists. They just hate their own leaders, that's all."

"These Arab leaders deserve it," Hadas said.

"Wow, strong words!" I responded.

"They are despots who deprive their people of their democracy and rights," Hadas said.

"And our leaders are perfect?" I said sarcastically.

"You have a president with a penchant for corruption and molestation," I said.

"He resigned," Hadas said.

"And we have a president who is trying to ram down healthcare on citizens who don't want it," I said.

"But Obama is trying to help people," Hadas said defensively.

"I agree," I said. "Obama has good intentions. He wants everyone to have healthcare. But you can't force that down on the citizens. It's just not the American way. Besides, American economy is not doing so well and the US government cannot pay for a healthcare system that will cover everyone. So, the plan is doomed from the start."

"That's not Obama's fault," Hadas said.

"You are right, but it is Obama's fault if he drives the country to the ground with the healthcare issue, knowing that it won't work," I said.

"But that's not happening, is it?"

"Well, it kind of is, unfortunately," I said. "Why do you think that there are new protest groups both in the Republican Party and the Democratic Party? The Republican Party has the Tea Party and the Democratic Party has the Occupy Wall Street Movement. Both are protests against the establishment."

"But Obama is not establishment," Hadas said.

"Of course, he is. He is the president. By definition, he is the establishment," I said.

"I guess you have a point, there," Hadas said.

"Okay, that makes three to two," I said. "I am only one point behind you, now!"

"Don't get too comfortable, little man," Hadas said. "You will soon see that the gap will increase."

"Like the gap between the rich and the poor in the United States of America?" I said.

"Even bigger," Hadas said.

"I don't think it can get bigger," I said. "Something like 1% of the population owns 90% of the nation's wealth."

"That is a problem," Hadas said.

"Well," I responded. "You know what the solution is?"

"No," Hadas said. "Tell me."

"Just make sure your kid goes to the Ivy League and becomes a part of the 1%"

"That's not a solution," Hadas said.

"Well, it is if you are currently in the 99% who owns the 10% of the wealth," I said.

"So, it is every man for himself, is it?" Hadas said.

"Well, you wanted democracy and capitalism," I said. "You will have to live with the good and the bad. That's life."

"Capitalism does not mean that there has to be income gap that big," Hadas said.

"Of course, it does," I said. "Capitalism is based on competition, and each is to receive according to how hard one works and achieves in one's life. If you want to get rid of the gap between the rich and the poor, then you have to espouse communism or Marxism. Are you prepared to do that?"

"Of course, not," Hadas said. "I like democracy."

"You cannot have your cake and eat it, too, as the saying goes in the USA," I said.

"What does that mean?" Hadas asked.

"It means that you cannot have everything you want in life," I said. "You have to choose. It's like with marriage. You may like two different guys in different ways, but you may like them both, but you can't marry them both."

Hadas responded, "That's why I would marry one and have the other guy as a lover on the side."

"Hadas, you are too much!" I said, laughing.

"After all, you guys do that, so why can't we, girls?" Hadas said.

"I agree with you," I said. "The system is unfair to women. Men can get away with having lovers and having affairs, but women can't. A guy who sleeps around in high school is cool and a stud, but a girl who sleeps around is a whore. That's unfair. I understand that."

Hadas said, "Yeah, it's so unfair."

"But that's life. You can't have your cake and eat it, too," I said.

"Will you stop saying that?" Hadas said. "I am going to hate cake from now on!"

"You know what will happen when your husband finds out about your lover?" I said.

"No," Hadas said with apprehension in her eyes.

"He is going to walk," I said.

"Walk?" Hadas asked.

"Walk away," I said.

"He will forgive me," Hadas said.

"I don't think so," I said. "Men are possessive, and they have male egos that do not allow for sharing of their woman."

"But my lover will be sharing me," Hadas said.

"But he's getting it for free, so he's not complaining, but that does not mean that he thinks of you as his partner," I said.

"That's so mean," Hadas said.

"That's just the way men are," I said. "And it's been that way since the stone ages."

Hadas responded, "I would like to think that we have evolved a bit since, then."

"Well, unfortunately, we don't seem to have," I said. "Evolution takes millions of years, remember. So, I don't think that things will change within next few million years."

"That's depressing," Hadas said.

"Not if you marry the one you love wholly and truly and madly and deeply," I said.

"When does it ever happen?" Hadas said.

"That's really cynical," I replied, as I realized my voice faltering "Of course, there is love and people love for love." I looked at Hadas. I felt a bit of uncertainty. "Don't they?"

"I don't know," Hadas said. "I think that you are a romantic. I am an Israeli, and we can't afford romance because there are Arab enemies all around us."

"Shhhhhh," I shushed her. "Don't you know? We are in an Arab bus, full of Arab people, headed to a completely Arab city."

"Now that you mention it," Hadas said. "What am I doing here?"

Oh, great! I began to think. Now, the woman is beginning to doubt. You know, there is nothing as horrible as when women begin to doubt. Do you think this relationship will work? Of course, honey, it will. But why? Why do you think this relationship will work? Because, honey, I love you and you love me. You sure? Are you really sure? Of course, honey. We against the world, baby. We against the world! Will you always be with me? Of course, honey. Will you never leave me? Of course, baby. Will you always love me? That goes without saying.

"You are here with a cool American guy for an adventure of your life time," I said. "After all, you are 'I want to see a revolution' Hadas, ain't you?"

Hadas started to flex her forearm. "That I am, sir. That I am."

"Oh, look at that muscle," I said. "It's not quite as big as your other roundness, but it's pretty big."

"Oh, Peter," Hadas rolled her eyes. "You can be so crass at times."

"Just calling it like it is," I said. "Don't hate me because I tell it like it is."

Hadas smiled and shook her head.

"I am going to take another nap," Hadas said.

"Another one?" I said. "I should just call you sleepy-head."

"Don't you dare," Hadas said, and she made a fist and started shaking it in my face. She was being playful, but her fist almost hit me on the nose, because the bus was moving relatively fast over uneven road.

"Hey, be careful, where you wave that stuff," I said.

"You are not afraid of being beat up by a little girl, are you?" Hadas said.

"I think I am going to catch some zzz's myself," I said. "Lai-lai-tov!"

"Lai-lai-tov!"

Chapter 6

"Peter, Peter," Hadas said, shaking me. "Wake up! We are here!

"Really?" I said, feeling dazed and confused. "Are we in Cairo?"

"It appears so," Hadas said in an understatement.

"That's cool," I said and forced myself awake.

"So, where are we going to go?" Hadas asked. "You prepared something for us, right?"

"Of course," I said. "I have this *Let's Go Egypt* guidebook, and that's all the preparation that we need!"

"Oh, you are like other guys," Hadas said. "So, unprepared!"

"No, I beg to differ," I said. "I know many guys who are extra-prepared and make all the reservations beforehand."

"Oh, so you are saying that I am not special enough for you to do that?" Hadas said in a typical female remonstration.

"Well, dear, I did not know you before," I said. She stared at me. "Well, not really, you know. And besides, this is more like an adventure, don't you think?"

"As long as we don't sleep in the street," Hadas complained.

"You are just afraid that I am going to sell you off to some Egyptian harem for 100 camels," I said, teasing her.

"Do you think that I would fetch that many camels?" Hadas said.

"At least 100 camels," I said, confidently.

"You are so sweet," Hadas said.

"Hey, I have an idea," I said. "Why don't we sell you for 100 camels, and then I will rescue you. We'll have 100 camels, and you will be back in my arms."

"Won't that make us like robbers?" Hadas asked.

"Just call us Bonnie and Clyde," I said.

"Who are they?" Hadas asked.

"Grasshopper, I have so much to teach you," I said.

"Talking about grasshopper, I am getting hungry," Hadas said. "Do you think we can get something to eat?"

"If talking about grasshopper makes you hungry, you have some issues, girl!" I said, trying to put on a serious face.

"Hey, grasshoppers are a delicacy in Africa," Hadas said.

"But we ain't in Africa," I said.

"Of course, we are in Africa," Hadas said. "Where do you think Egypt is?"

"Oh," I said, "You are right."

"Of course, I am right," Hadas said. "Who's the grasshopper now?"

"Me grasshopper," I said, "And you eat me."

"Huh?" Hadas said.

"I tried to do that Me Tarzan and You Jane bit, but with a different twist."

Hadas said, "It doesn't work."

"Okay, now for that grasshopper delicacy," I said and started to go toward the exit of the bus. Hadas followed. We grabbed our bags and realized that we were in desperate need of a toilet. None was there. So, of course, my attention turned to finding a hotel.

"Screw the *Let's Go Egypt*!" I said. "Let's go to that place which says, 'Hotel.'"

"If it has a bathroom, it's fine with me," Hadas said.

We both scurried toward the billboard and building. It was a small building, but it looked clean enough. When we entered the reception, and asked for a room, the receptionist said, "One room left."

"How much?" I asked.

"Ten dollars," he said.

"Did you say 10 dollars?" I asked. "Is that like 10 US dollars?"

"Yes," he said.

"I like this place already," I said to Hadas. Hadas rolled her eyes.

"We want the room," I said and paid 10 dollars in cash. And the receptionist gave us the key. When we went to the room, it was a simple room without any desks. There was just one bed in the center of the room and drawers. The room was about 80% bed, and the bed was smack in the middle. I noticed Hadas turning red.

"Hey, at least, we know we'll get good sleep," I said.

"But there is only one bed," Hadas said.

"You are not going to be a baby about this, are you?" I said. "We are both adults. You sleep on that side and I sleep on this side."

Hadas looked at me, but I could not read her thoughts.

"While you are thinking, I am going take a shower," I said and went to a small, dingy room right next to the bedroom, which had a toilet and a shower.

"Wait!" Hadas said. "Let me go to the bathroom, first."

"Okay," I said. Hadas went in and took some time. And then she emerged from the bathroom with her head lowered, like a poodle who had her fur shaved for the summer.

"Oh, God!" I said. "It smells like the dead Pharaoh came back to life and took a crap in there after eating a whole jar of beans and onions."

Hadas looked away and did not say anything.

"God! I can't breathe!" I said. "I am suffocating in here."

Hadas said, "Will you just stop it!"

I was afraid that she was going to start crying, so I just closed the bathroom door and took my shower. The shower was remarkably strong. It felt good with water bouncing off of my body. I looked at my skin and marveled at bouncing water. I put my finger on my arm and pressed it, and I could see a pressure mark. For some reason, that fascinated me. I must have been very tired.

"That felt good!" I said as I opened the bathroom door.

It looked like Hadas was mad.

"Do you want to take shower, next?" I asked.

"Okay," Hadas said, and went in to the bathroom.

I felt fatigue, so I just slipped into my side of the bed. I meant to stay there in a comfortable position, but fell asleep. I don't know how long I have been sleeping, but I was stirred awake. I could swear that I felt someone jumping up and down on the bed near where I was, but I figured that the feeling was just a dream. Why would anyone jump up and down on the bed next to me? And besides, only Hadas was in the room. And I could not imagine Hadas jumping up and down on the bed like a 4 year old. When all cleared, and I could see Hadas, she was sitting on her side of the bed.

"You want to hear the weirdest thing?" I asked.

"What?" Hadas acted like she didn't notice me.

"I thought I felt someone jumping up and down on the bed," I said.

Hadas was sitting on her side of the bed and threw me a look. There was a gleam in her eyes. "I don't know what you are talking about. It was probably just a dream."

"You are probably right," I said. Then, it dawned on me that she was wearing a white shirt and short shorts. I don't think she was wearing anything under her shirt, although I was not going to go and feel her shirt to confirm this. Her shirt had a love sign in the front and read, "I love you." Such a girly shirt! And her shorts were pink. I did not even know that Israelis even had pink colored clothing, let alone pink shorts for a girl that was way too short to be wearable in any place but the beach. I don't know if she was wearing anything underneath that, but I wasn't going to ask.

I felt awake. I didn't think that I could go back to sleep again. I was a bit upset by this, but then my discontentment was absorbed by the sight of apparently curvaceous female form of Hadas in skimpy clothing within arm's reach away from me.

"Hadas," I said, "You look really cute in that outfit."

"You think so?" Hadas asked in feigned innocence.

"Yeah, I do," I said. "You look really cute."

"I am surprised that I do because I am sore all over from the bus ride."

"Didn't shower relieve your stress?" I said.

"Actually, the shower made me feel the soreness even more," Hadas said. "And I feel, so sore. And I am aching so much."

"You know," I said. "If you want, I can give you a massage. Maybe, it will help relieve your soreness."

"You think?" Hadas said in a slightly shaky voice.

"Yeah, I do," I said. "I think you will feel so much better."

"Really?" Hadas asked with her eyes wide.

"Yeah, I do." I said. "I actually took massage class in college, so you are looking at a professional."

"Are you that good?" Hadas asked.

"Well, you can find out in a second," I said. "Come over here."

"Okay," Hadas said, and she moved closer to me.

"I am going to lean against the wall, and then you lean against me."

"Okay," Hadas said.

I leaned against the wall, so that my back was pressed against the wall. I was sitting with my body perpendicular with my legs, flat on the bed. I moved my legs away from each other, to make a docking station for Hadas, who seemed to understand this function. Hadas moved her back towards me, and I felt her hair begin to brush against my face. It smelled like rose pedals in a spring day. I could feel the gentle softness of her hair touching my face, and I felt a kind of excitement pervade through my body.

Hadas slowly leaned her body against mine, and I could feel her back pressuring my front torso. It felt good. I guess she was a bit tired, so she pressed against me harder than she had intended, but I was not about to complain about that.

I placed both of my hands on her neck. I felt that that was the best place to start touching her. I felt the gentle smoothness of her neck on both of my hands. With my right hand, I gently stroked her right side of the neck. And with my left hand, I stroked her left neck.

"Your neck feels a bit tense," I said.

"Hmmm," she sighed.

I gently held her neck in my hands, and then applied pressure to her neck through my fingers. I could feel the texture of the bones in her neck, and I tried to stroke them gently. I let my hands completely cover her neck for a few minutes and used my thumbs to apply gentle pressure to the back of her neck. Slowly, I undulated the movement of my thumbs so that the back of her neck received evened pressure from top to bottom. All the while, I was applying gentle pressure to her front of the neck with my pointing fingers and index fingers. I thought that I felt the purring of her neck, but it might have been my imagination.

Slowly, I moved my pointing fingers up, above the neck capacity. I felt the shape of her jaws and followed its contours with my pointing fingers. I raised my thumb higher as well, and slowly felt the lower orb of her ears. I put my thumb in the back of her earlobe and pointing finger in the front of her ear lobe and exerted gentle pressure. It felt a bit cold, but I could feel it quickly warm up. I moved my thumb up behind her earlobe and traced the contours of her ears. With my pointing fingers, I traced the visible frontsides of her ears.

I allowed my hand, then, to slide over her cheeks. I felt the smoothness of her cheeks, and slowly allowed my fingers to follow the contours of her nose. Slowly, the fingers moved down toward her lips, and I used primarily my right index finger to trace the contours of her lips. Her lips felt full under my finger. I thought that she opened her lips a little bit, because one of my fingers accidently felt her teeth as I tried to trace the contours of her lips. I thought I heard small sound coming out of her, but I was not sure, because I was fixed on giving her pleasure.

Her head began to lean against me, and soon, her head was leaning against my left shoulder. I felt the fullness of her hair, and I was drunk on the effusion of aroma from her hair. But I was also suffocating from the profusion of her hair that inundated my face. I felt my sense of balance lost, as I felt the fullness of her body and her odors engulf me in a torrent of longing. As her neck rested on my shoulders, I could not but help noticing the beautiful, curvaceous mounds of her upper torso heaving like mountains, ready for volcanic activity. I noticed the peak of her mountains protruding enticingly like red popsicle sticks against her white shirt. As her shirt stretched against her leaning body, the white shirt stuck relentlessly against her chest and made a stamp-like imprint of its form. I could see her very curves and undulation, hills and the valleys, protrusions and intrusions. And as I marveled at her veiled topography of her body, I could feel the excitement felt by landscapers who survey the land to be developed and to be enjoyed. I eyed the beautiful topography in front of me and imagined where everything should go to extract the maximum pleasure for the land, as land is alive and has feelings, as Native Americans have long taught us. The land breathes and feels. The land feels pleasure and pain. The land wants to be free, yet desired to be tamed. The land wants to be left alone like a cat drinking her Vitamin-D milk; yet, the land wants to be touched, like a cat purring with desire and longing. The land wants to be ignored, so that she could have her independence, but the land longs to be fettered to the one whom she loves. The land wants to be alone sometimes, but the land desires to be filled and full with what she wants on her topography. I surveyed the land before me and the undulating hills that had life of their own. And I imagined where everything should go and in what order as a ping-pong player plans to execute a strategy on the ball that is flying at him. How he returns the projectile will result in his victory or loss. And I did not want to presume that the victory was won, that the land was already conquered.

The land has to be respected. The topography should be appreciated for its beauty as well as its form. There was delicate balance to be had. To enjoy the land fully, one had to talk to it, to be sensitive to it, to be conscious of its needs and desires. One cannot force oneself upon the land and experience the maximum pleasure that could be derived from the land. The land is filled with boundless pleasure and energy that can be tapped. Limitless is the ability to enjoy and to feel. But the land can only be harnessed as far as the imagination of the one who is taking stock of it. The land can only be enjoyed insofar as it wills itself to be enjoyed. The land has to give itself and surrender itself of its own will and volition so that there is nothing left but abnegation and desire to give itself. To bring the land to that state of longing and desire, that state of conscious willingness and self-giving, one cannot take the land for granted. The land is alive with feelings and self-determining will. The land can change its mind with the change of the wind.

As Hadas' head rested on my shoulders and as I felt the dependence on me that her resting head revealed, I knew that it did not necessarily promise her giving up of herself fully to me, without reservation and without doubt. I knew that it was uncertain until the moment that was given possession of it by itself.

I stroked her hair and began to massage the upper part of her torso. I felt the constraints of her shirt and wanted to damn her shirt. It was like a barrier that kept true appreciation at bay. There was a cover on the convertible that denied full enjoyment of a convertible driving in the open road with wind flowing through the opened torso of the car. Wind caressing every naked part of the convertible body. Headlights hitting the wind and making the wind cry out in shrill pleasure. Why should the convertible be covered up like that? Why was Hadas' convertible covered up by this white shirt? One piece of clothing that prevented the full enjoyment of the convertible ride in the wind, with wind shrilling out in pleasure. White sheet covering the convertible.

I did not want the joyride to be stopped by one piece of clothing. I wanted her to feel. I wanted her to enjoy. And I wanted to see her with her desire satisfied. I wanted to see her enjoying her ecstasy. So, I slowly began to move my right hand down her neck. At that moment, I felt one of her hands grab my other hand that was resting at her side. Hadas took my left hand, and she placed that hand on top of her left breast. I could feel the curves of her breasts in my hands, even though there was a piece of clothes between my hand and her bare, naked breasts. And I could feel the protrusion of her nipple in my hand. With my four fingers, I cupped her left breast, and with my thumb, I pressed her nipple, as if it were a button that was to be pushed. I felt the hardened nipple underneath the thin Isreali-made T-Shirt, and I said in my mind, "Thank you Israeli T-Shirt makers, for your flimsy, bad quality T-Shirts." If the T-Shirt had been American-made, I probably would not have been able to feel anything underneath her white shirt.

I don't think that Hadas did not find this unpleasurable, because I could see on her face a sensation of the sublime. She was in the clouds of pleasure, and the sublime enjoyment was written in her face, filled with desire, yet with a sense of sereneness.

Naturally, I did not want her single mound to feel jealous at the other occupied mound. Thus, I brought my right hand over to the lonely, standing-alone mound that was eagerly waiting to be asked for the next dance. May I have this dance? I did not ask. I saw, I went, and I conquered. Let's have this dance, and the hand moved into its place. And the hand was dancing on the mound and with the mound. In a twin movement of the pair of hands, both of the mounds were being handled, sometimes genteelly and at other times with little more show of emotion.

All this time, her head was resting on my shoulder with her eyes closed, as if she wanted to enjoy the sensations. She did not want to talk. She did not want to see. She just wanted to feel. And feel I did, her beautiful upper torso. But like all things, pleasure begs to be shared. And as such, the pleasure could not be confined to the hills. The valleys and the plains had to be satiated as well. It would be remiss of the landscape artist to develop the hills and leave the valleys and the plains before it wanting and needing. I was going to satisfy that want. I was going to satiate that need. Thus, I allowed my hands to trickle down from the acme of the two mountains towards the plains underneath. I felt the tenderness of her stomach underneath the white shirt. I was getting used to the texture of the white shirt. Israeli T-shirt might be cheap, but it was perfect for this type of activity. I would not swear, but I think that the thin T-shirt rubbing against her body gave her a type of sensation that she hadn't felt before, especially in light of the fact that her synapses were shooting messages at the speed of light. This is pleasurable. This feels good. What feels good must be right.

Little beknownst to me, the quick sending of messages was clouding her judgment and inhibitions. I could see her abdomen relax before my hands, even as periodic spasms entered her being. And her previously tightly closed legs seemed to have relaxed and opened its gates with poorly-suppressed alacrity. I did not know what to make of the message sent by her body. Was there miscommunication between her cognitive process and her emotional desire? Which message is the right one? The confusion seems to be within her being, and it seemed as if her desire had killed all common sense and cognitive deduction. There she was with her abdominal muscles periodically undulating and her legs completely relaxed as if she had taken some laxative.

I felt a clammy coldness in my hands as I felt a sudden nervousness enter me. I felt a kind of fear intermixed with desire. I wanted to touch the pink shorts, but I felt a bit of hesitation. I could feel that my hands were feeling clammy. Sometimes, a piece of clothing can be a good thing. As I continued to massage her abdomen with patience, I realized that it was no longer patience that sustained my gentle, continued massage of her abdomen. It was hesitation.

There is a saying in the USA. "One who hesitates is lost." And that phrase just flashed before my mind's eye as if it were lit on neon lights. One who hesitates is lost. One who hesitates is lost.

And I allowed my hand to go down lower and lower in her abdominal track. One part of me wanted something to block my path. My head was dizzy with desire, and I thought I was going to lose consciousness. I felt nervousness that seemed to immobilize me. And it did not help that a part of my body seemed to have fallen asleep under the pressure of her leaning body. I wondered how long we have been that way. I don't think that I had felt such protracted time of nervous pleasure in my life. Often, intimate encounters were short and quick. But this was prolonged. I wondered if my body could handle such a prolonged sense of pleasure that was wanting and wanting and was not satisfied. How long can you wait for the satiation? How long can Penelope wait? Apparently, forever. But obviously, Odysseus could not, and that is why he returned. I felt like Odysseus, who could not wait. And I wondered if Penelope could wait forever. I guess I was forcing Penelope to wait as

Odysseus had done. But the prolonged wait added a sensation that was unique. I felt pleasure that felt like pain. I felt pleasure that felt like fear. My nervous system was so excited that it could not distinguish between pain and pleasure, fear and happiness. All was merged into one. And it felt good.

So, I did not want to rush. Of course, satiation could be deeply satisfying, but it was short and quick. In the current state, with the patience of Hadas and apparently my patience, I could feel protracted unique pleasure. I did not want to rush it to end.

How often in my life will I meet a woman who was patient enough to allow me to enjoy this limbo pleasure for hours on end? Something tells me that not many women would allow me this luxury. "Honey, just get it over with! I am tired." I wonder how many men hear this line.

Here I was in a sublime moment that may be the only moment in my life that I feel such a protracted, confused sense of desire and longing. Certainly, I was not going to rush it. I was going to savor the moment. I was going to linger.

That sounds all nice and good, but I did not account for one thing. The animal side of a man. Every man has an animal side. Call it the primal side. The Me Tarzan, You Jane factor. Wham bam, thank you ma'am. It is just 4 minutes?

It is the primal desire that takes hold, and the man becomes an animal. Yes, it's over in 4 minutes, but insofar as the man is concerned, he got what he wanted. After all, a man can climax only once at any time, and everything before that is nothing compared to the final climax. So, whether it takes 4 minutes to get there or 1 minute or 1 hour, the goal is the end, the touchdown. The 3 shot score. For a man, shorter is better, because everything is meant to lead up to that final moment. Everything before that is kind of boring for the animalistic man.

The animal can take over. And the animal does not care about foreplay. The animal does not care about pleasuring the woman. The animal only cares about the end climax. And when that animal takes over, it is a quick dash to the finish line. Hell to the woman's wishes! Hell to pleasuring the woman! I am just going to get some.

The fastfood culture of the United States may add to the detraction of pleasure from the American woman. But it is not just the American man. All men are wired as animals. And they just want that trophy at the end. Nothing else matters. How the game is played does not matter that much. Yeah, they say it matters, but in truth it doesn't matter. It's all about the end trophy. Everything is to build up to that and is for that.

I felt my animalistic side overpowering me. And I wished that I could just enjoy her in my heightened sense of emotion and feeling. I knew how precious that was. But then, I also felt the tugging at my male member. It was beginning to hurt. It actually hurt for God's sake!

Maybe men are not biologically designed to enjoy protracted pleasure. They are just meant to consummate the deal. Do the deed. Let the champagne pop out of the bottle. Don't hold the bottle forever, dude! Don't you know what you are there for? Pop the bottle open! Pop that cherry! What are you doing looking at it and admiring it? What are you? Some kind of a Nancy? Just pop it!

The male culture is built on man's biological dictates. Man cannot just enjoy the feeling and emotion, for the desire will turn into actual physical aching when near a naked woman. Okay, Hadas was not naked, but her nakedness was only one sheet of clothing away, and I could feel her nakedness beneath that thin, cheaply, Israeli made clothing. So, the male mind kicks in and the messages are sent from the brain that it is time to shoot that soccer ball into the net. Hey, dude, there are no goalies. What ya doing? Just kick it in! You have a clear shot to the goal!

Aching pain. Why? Because it was supposed to have fired a long time ago. You are a couple hours too late! What if it misfires, dude? Don't miss your timing! Foreplay is for faggots!

What? Foreplay is for faggots?

Yes, foreplay is for faggots! You don't want your girl going around telling people that you spend an inordinate time on foreplay, because if any man hears that, he's going to assume that you are a fucking faggot. So, don't be a fag about it, just shoot it in! Thus, the barbarian male choir chimes in.

Man's biology seems to agree, however, because it does really hurt when it is not released in time. The load was not meant to be carried by the little guy for so long. The load, which was loaded, is meant to be fired. So, unload your burden, dude!

Yes, you can hear the biological dictate. But the biological dictate isn't everything, is it? If you have a time when a woman wants to be foreplayed for hours and hours and you can enjoy the desire and the emotions for her for hours and hours and hours without actually consummating, why should you not indulge? Do you think that it is easy for the woman to be so patient and to enjoy your hand on her body for so long without intercourse? Does that not mean something? Maybe she's into you for you and not just for the little guy with the load that has to be unloaded. Why should you give up on that when you have the moment? Do you think that moment comes around, every day?

What makes a woman want someone so much that it consumes her being? What makes a woman want to be next to someone, just to be next to someone, for hours and hours? What makes a woman want to be touched and touched and be touched again? This is the mystery of life, because no one can adequately explain why such a state of mind and emotion exists in some woman.

A woman can be married to a man and want the occasional sex because it is pleasurable, but does that woman want her husband to just keep touching her, hour after hour? Well, you try and see and see what happens.

Women are like cats, and they do not generally want to be touched. They want the pleasure. Yes. Who doesn't want the pleasure? But pleasure is different from intimate longing. Sometimes, women are lonely, and they want a boyfriend or a husband. But that is different from desiring someone. Obviously, from a man's point of view, it doesn't really make any difference. "Hey, dude, I am getting' some." "Yeah, that's so cool dude!" "You getting' some?" "Well, my old lady's been like, 'I am tired and shit.'" "Hey, dude, that sucks." Yep, this is the extent of male assessment on relationships. Men are simple, animalistic creatures. And their capacity for orgasm is once and for about 10 seconds. After they ejaculate, they cannot physically get it up again for a few hours. And since men are animalistic and are focused on the climax, they don't really care why their woman is with them. All they care about is (1) they are with them, and (2) that they are getting some. Nothing else really matters for men. Yes, men can be domesticated to a certain extent, but men generally retain their animalistic side.

Women are different. They actually care about love, and they care about feelings and emotions. It is always the woman who goes out of their way to satisfy. Men even forget their woman's birthday, even if they have been married for decades. Men can be pathetic. But what can you do, when men are all like that?

"You are like a woman," one of my female friends told me. You can imagine that I was not necessarily happy to hear this, although coming from a female person, I recognize that it could be a compliment.

"How so?" I asked.

"You care that I have pleasure," she said. She was a friend with whom I had become intimate.

You can imagine that it was an awkward moment. Not really, but I think that's the right thing to say.

I tried to ignore my little member in pain. No pain, no gain, right?

I felt Hadas' abdomen. By this time, she turned around to kiss me. She did not really open her eyes. She opened them for a bit to locate my face, so she would not be kissing my nose. As soon as she located my lips, she kissed me on the lips. I had my hand on her abdomen, and she was writhing on my body as she turned to kiss me. This did not help my little member, which felt additional excitement and pain. Hadas kissed me, and it was very, very wet. It is like she unleashed her saliva onto my lips.

And I don't know how it happened. But as soon as I started to kiss her, I felt her tongue fire and shoot into my mouth. And her tongue was swimming inside my mouth, as if an exhibitionist swimmer was taking a skinny dip in front of those whom she imagined to be desiring her body. The tongue swam inside the pool of my mouth, as if it possessed it. Strangely, I did not dislike the sensation caused by her writhing tongue. I started to suck on her tongue, but felt that that was too gay, so I stopped. I could have imagined it to be a like big nipple, but even with a big imagination, that was stretching it. So, I just let my tongue dance next to hers, like a manly man dance with a delicate flower female. A very heterosexual dance! Yes, hip-hop dance. Who's heard of a gay hip-hop artist? Hop-hop music is innately homophobic. Hey, best song to dance the heterosexual dance to! And I let my very masculine tongue dance the hip hop with Hadas's very female tongue. And there was no sucking, after the initial inadvertent, I-did-not-know-better suck of her tongue. If there was going to be any sucking, it was going to be on her part, because that's not gay at all. Obviously!

She seemed overwhelmed by the kiss. I often asked myself, if men and women feel differently when kissing. Yeah, I like to kiss beautiful women. It feels good. But I don't get all excited from kissing. What excites me is a woman with nice, shapely breasts, and not-too-big-but-not-too-small butt wearing a

ss, it's not the best example of how puzzling some things
 out; I guess it's your fuckin' fault.
Oh, how about this example? You like a girl and you are nice
er. And then, she's like, Ah, you are like my little brother. I
love you. And you try to touch her, and she says: Ah, that's
weet. And she pushes your hand away. What happened?
haven't you heard that song, "She fuckin' hates me!"? The
goes something like, "I was too nice and now she fuckin'
me." Yep, being nice can be a liability when it comes to
en. Haven't you heard the phrase? Nice guys finish last.
was referring to nice guys in their relationship with girls.
d if you think that nice girls are different? Well, you are
 fuckin' bigger schmuck than you had ever thought of
elf, aint you? Nice girls are bitches just like bad girls. Girls
ls. This may sound male chauvinistic and shit, and don't
ing people – I mean girls – I said this shit, because you
they have a cow and shit. But I ain't shittin' you when I
e girls are worse, sometimes.
kin' eh! Don't you fuckin' remember high school? Shit!
ent to college and did too much dope that you forget
appened like five fuckin' years ago. Shit. You fucked up.
et me refresh your fucked-up brain what happened in
hool. Yeah, there was this nice girl from a nice family.
 always clean-cut and wore preppy clothes. She talked
bing to church and shit. And you are like, fuck, this girl
per! So, you start being all nice and shit because you
at that's what she'll want. And she keeps saying, You
 a nice guy! And you are like, fuck, this is happening!
appening to me! You get all excited and shit. And you
t you are going out, when you are just hanging out.
 you are an item, but all she's thinking is, He be my
 you are like, I have no clue. Fuck, she's an angel! No,
n' dope! She's your fuckin' devil! She's like the
f Beelzebub. She's like Satanic bitch want to be. And
she is all innocent and shit. But how do you know

thong, sitting in an elegant, yet suggestive pose that is not too crass. That actually excites me, like it would every other man. Men are excited from looking.

Kissing a girl. Yeah, that feels nice, but that doesn't really excite the way that a pink thong does on a nice curvaceous female body that is not shown off too crudely. Okay, a 18-year-old, 5'10' with 110 pounds with blonde hair and blue eyes with a Swedish accent, from Stockholm, could not do anything crass even if she wanted to, but such a nymph is every man's exception to the crass rule. But you get the point.

For a woman, good kissing can be a religious experience, it seems. Sometimes, women start to moan when they kiss. Sometimes, you have to ask yourself, "Are you fucking kidding me?" But I think that not everyone is shitting you. I think that some women actually feel a kind of sexual pleasure from kissing. I ain't going to take a nationwide poll, so don't ask me to. But I don't think I am wrong in saying this. Hey, maybe I am naïve, and if I am wrong, you can call me naïve and slap me silly, but you see, that's how confident I feel – that for some women, kissing can be a religious experience. I tell you. I have felt some women writhing their body against mine after kissing me. Some wrap their body tightly around me like a Brazilian snake that wraps you and squeezes you to death. I can't see things from a woman's perspective, since I am a guy, but I think they see kissing differently from the way we men see it. I guess for men, this may remain one of those mysteries of life. Oh, well!

Hadas seemed deeply satisfied by the kissing, and she turned back to her previous position. I guess she wanted to be touched a bit more. At least, that's how I interpreted things. Hadas writhing on my body had heightened my sense of being, and the excitement led me quickly toward my animalistic side. I slid my hand down from her abdomen toward the well-spring of her bodily oasis. The dry desert that produces the rejuvenating liquid that springs up, which carries the sweetness of her inner being. With the palm branches surrounding the oasis, the sweet aroma filled oasis was waiting for someone who would eagerly lap its essence.

The pink neon shorts seem to cheapen the experience on one level. But on the other hand, pink is a passionate color, and it matched the passion that was joining Hadas and me in a mixture of ecstasy. My hand inched slowly but surely toward its goal. Inch by Inch. Bit by bit. Like a spider that is forming a web. Like Charlotte's web that opens a whole world of understanding and experiences, my hand weaved an invisible web on her body. Like a Spiderman's web wrapping a criminal body in spider web in order to capture him, my invisible web wrapped Hadas's body and claimed her for myself. And my hand now was inching toward the prize, the juicy, tasty fly that is caught in the middle of the web.

Chapter 7

It is puzzling how things turn out
Sometimes, what you least expect hap
have a best friend and you have a girl
are eager that they get along. So, you e
that your best mate and your best g
happens? They do the wild thing. Th
And what do they say? Ah, it just hap
this thing to happen, bud. Fuck you
fuckin' asshole! But honey, I am
understand how you can just fall in l
fucking bitch! You didn't fall in lo
fuckin' vagina just created a big cra
fuckin' slut! It's like, here's the goa
just bring the ball right up to the
Fucking, Joseph, Mary, and the ani
manger 2,000 years ago! What do
idiot?

Yes, but such things happen.
the schmuck? You are, for letting
bond and be alone and fuck ea

that I am right? She goes out with that big asshole, who keeps calling you a fuckin' nerd, like in front of everyone, intentionally to humiliate you.

And what happens when you tell her about it? Ah, you are the best, your best friend? Who you think is your lover, even though you have never held her hand for more than like a fraction of a second? She starts laughing. Then, she tries to suppress her laugher. This makes it worse, of course. Then, while visibly trying to repress her laughter, but still laughing, she says, He's just joking with you. Take this joke you fuckin' bitch! Did you know that your ass is way too big for your height, you fucking wide-ass-bitch! Did you fuckin' know that you are flatter than the plains of the Plains Indians! Yeah, you heard me. Well, actually, she did not hear you because you were saying these things in your head. What you actually said after the debacle is a nice guy response. Yeah, you are probably right. He is a funny guy. That's probably why that asshole is doin' her while you are her biatch, never to even touch her. Yeah, you nice guy piece of shit! Stop doing the drugs and just wake up! Nice guys finish last.

Why are you looking at this page like an idiot? Because you don't believe me? Yeah, just try to think back at your high school. Just bring those repressed memories back, dude, and you know that I tell you honest-to-God truth.

It's puzzling how things turn out because you are fuckin' repressing your memories from high school. High school is good for two things. One, high school is good for learning what not to do. Don't be that nice guy to that hot chick. You ain't getting' some? You still haven't learned? Then, why did you hell go to high school. You should have dropped out of high school and made something of yourself. Like Bill Gates. Okay, he dropped out of Harvard, but you get my point.

Second, high school is good for learning to evade the ire of the authorities and get away with shit. What? You haven't learn this? Maybe, that's why you get caught at every wrong thing you do and are always paying fine after fine. Dude, learn the shit in high school that you should learn! If you wanted to learn the book stuff, then you should have gone to a high school in China or Korea or some other fuckin' Asian country. They actually teach you the subjects and book knowledge and shit. American high schools basically have "C" students teaching you because they would otherwise be unemployed if they did not become a teacher. They did not have high enough grades to get into the Ivy League, and they were not sporty enough to become a construction worker or a police man. So, these losers became teachers. You ain't learning shit in American high schools. Have you talked to some Paki guy who studied in a Pakistani high school? He knows shit. Lots of shit. Have you asked the same questions of someone who went to an American high school? He can't answer shit. But you know why it's worth it to go to an American high school? Because that nice Paki shit will do shit in America, because he did not learn the two important points that you can really only learn in an American high school: don't be a nice guy to hot chicks and learn to evade authority while making them think that they are in charge.

Consider a Paki guy in the American workplace? He's actually going to do shit and work. Yeah, you know what I mean. You have seen such dweebish Pakis in your company. They do shit. Lot's of shit. Just to impress the manager. And the manager is like: Shit, I have a fuckin' Paki who makes me look bad. Fuck this Paki and fuck Pakistan! We should just nuke the whole Paki nation and exterminate all the Pakis who are going to make Americans look bad. You know what I mean. Because of this Paki who went to a Pakistani high school, now, the manager has to pretend harder that he is working, or his boses will be like, Your Paki worker does more work than you. You make Americans look bad. You see why we are losing to Asia?

And you will be like, You fuckin' asshole. We are not losing to Pakistan. We are losing to India. Get your fuckin' countries straight. He's not from India. He's from fuckin' Pakistan. But you won't say that out loud. After all, mamma raised no fool. You ain't gonna get yourself fired, are you?

But consider this. Let's say that your boss could hear your thoughts. He'll be like. Like, whatever! That Bombay guy from India in Marketing is just like this Paki in Sales. They put us to shame! No wonder these Chinks are beating us. And you will be like, You fuckin' asshole, the Indian guy in Marketing was born in Atlanta, Georgia. Technically, he's not a Chink, because "Chink" is a derogatory, racist name-calling for those of Chinese background. Of course, you are not going to say this out loud. But let's say that your boss could hear what you are thinking. He'll be like. You fuckin' piece of shit, who can be fired with a drop of my snot. I know he's not a fuckin' Chink. But I don't know a derogatory, racist name-calling for an Indian. So, I fuckin' substituted one racist name for an Asian group and transferred its racist power to the Indian guy. So, fuck you, who is worse than a Paki!

Obviously, you did not get the memo! You did not get your money's worth in high school. What's that? You went to a public school? It was free? No, schmuck. It's not free. Taxes. Property taxes. Income taxes. State taxes. All the shit taxes fund your school. And you did not get your fuckin' money's worth! You did not learn the important second point. You have to evade authority while making the authority think that they have control. What you should have fuckin' done when you had a Paki who went to a Paki high school working like an eager beaver in your department is to transfer the fuckin' Paki ass back to Pakistan. If you can't pull it off because you did not learn enough shit in high school, then you should try to have him transferred to Marketing, so the Indian Chink and the Paki will make your buddy manger at Marketing look bad, then you are a shoo-in for the promotion. You can eliminate your competition. The Marketing Manager probably will be laid off or replaced by the Paki or the Indian Chink. You know, every company has to have like a token Indian Chink or a Paki or an actual Chink in management to prove to the federal government that they are in compliance with non-discrimination laws. You don't have to be the Jesus who takes up his own cross and die. Shit, that was some stupid shit! Dying for a sorry ass disciple, like Peter, who denies him three times as he goes to his death. I wouldn't have died for him. I would have been like. You fuckin' Peter! You gonna deny me after all I have done for you? Upon this rock I wish smash your brain, and let Hannibal Lector eat your scattered brains with a straw! You fuckin' go to the cross! That's what I would have done. None of this be-Jesus shit.

Yeah, eliminate the Asian guy and you are home free. Hire some black dude who is on a long recovery program from his slavery days. He'll have to make up for loss time by his ancestors, so you know he'll be doin' no shit. Just listening to hip hop music on his iPod and pretending like he was listening to some white music to impress the KKK bosses. Affirmative Action Columbia Degree. Worth shit! But you know what this black guy has over you? He learned shit in high school he needed to. But he's not going to be much of a threat because most white people hate black people, subconsciously. They tell themselves consciously that they like black people. And maybe they believe it because their fantasy football pick is black, but when it comes down to it, their subconscious don't lie. So, you being white, you have no threat from the lazy black worker.

How about the Mexican? Okay, he's not from Mexico. He's from Columbia or Bolivia or Honduras or one of those obscure countries in Latin America. But I tell you what. They are all Mexican to me. They all speaka Spanish and shit. And eat some thing that resembles human feces. Brown and shit. So, they are all Mexican and shit to me. But don't tell anyone that I said that. You know these Mexicanos are all sensitive and shit, and they will get all pissed. But you know he's no habla English and won't get the promotion that you will. The Mexicano is probably an illegal, any way. And the anti-Mexicano direction of the Gringos in the USA? He's no fuckin' threat to you!

Can I hear the choir sing, "Chee-chee Chong!" or "Shaka Kahn!"? Shaka Kahn! Shaka Kahn! Shaka Kahn! Chee-chee Chong!"

Mexicanos may be no problem for you, but the the Paki and the Indian Chink – they are there to take your job. They are your threat. So, get them deported back to Pakistan. Plant some weed or shit. That sometimes works. If you are too chicken to plant something on his desk? Just find him making like one mistake and then run with it, a like Heisman trophy winner. Hey, it may be small, like taking 2 minutes longer on a coffee break. Yeah, he had the diarrhea because you put stuff in his coffee before offering it to him. But that 2 minutes are precious. It's your ticket to upper management. Mr. Vice President. Doesn't that sound good? Don't let a Paki take that away from you! Haven't you learned what you needed to learn in high school? Why the hell did you go to high school for? Fuck, you learned shit in high school!

Yeah, damn right, no fuckin' Paki or Indian Chink can survive in the American workplace, because they did not go to the American high school. It's like boot camp for survival in the USA. Harvard fuckin' degree? Fuckin' useless in the hands of a Paki or an Indian Chink who went to high school in some fuckin' corner of Asia where they eat only vegetables. Fuckin' Vegans! Eat like a cow, be treated like a cow! Now, did I commit a blasphemy to your god? To quote an American president, "Wouldn't be prudent!" But you have to do the wild thing, once in a while. Do the wild thing! Wild thing! Screw prudent!

But did I tell you how much I hate Vegans? If humans were not meant to eat animals, then they would not be here on earth, would they? But I digress.

It's important to learn what you need to learn at the stage that you need to learn it. If you went to a high school in China or in Korea, go back to your country! Because you have no fuckin' chance for success in the USA! This is God Bless America for the weed-smokers and the under-aged drinkers. Ain't no squeaky clean, praying five times per day Paki gonna survive the USA!

But it's puzzling how things turn out. As if it is not bad enough that we have like Pakis to make us look bad in our own country, now we have all these fuckin' Asian countries that make America look bad. Shit, what do these people eat? Why are they like fuckin' overtaking us?

Well, I have a theory on this shitty circumstance. Not enough American high school students are learning what they need to in high school. All this anti-bullying zero tolerance laws by some fuckin' Jewish principals who have flashbacks of their own nerdy high school experiences of being proffered wedges have made red-blooded American high schools into a bunch of faggots who do not know how to survive. Boys will be boys. If he looks like a nerd, of course he will get his head bashed in a few times a week. This is America, God-damn it!

When was America great? When the Jocks were allowed to beat the nerds. It taught people the biology of life. Predators and the prey. The survival of the fittest. Now, with all this PC shit and zero tolerance and fuckin' ferry Obama policies against bullying, we are creating a nation of faggots who cannot compete in the world. You think that Chinese jocks are not beating up on Chinese nerds? They probably use nasty Kung-Fu shit, too! Of course, those Chinks are going to have a survival instinct greater than our children.

Why don't you send out soldiers without boot camp and training for battle? Do you think that they will win? How are American boys going to beat Indian Chinks and Pakis in global economic competition, if they have been fuckin' Obama-sanitized with zero tolerance policies against bullies? It's like being in a zoo. You think that a lion who has been in a zoo all his life is going to survive in the wild? Hell, no! So, how do you suppose these fuckin' faggots in bully-free American high schools are going to survive in the world? Of course, not! And that is why America is losing its competitive edge. That's why Chinks and Indian Chinks and their countries are beating us.

What makes it worse is that we have these imports in our companies, like spies and infiltrators, tainting our workplace with such poisons, like working without surfing during work hours. Fuck, it is our right as American citizens to use company time and money and internet recourses to surf the net and engage in social networking, like Facebook! How else are we going to inflate the value of social networking companies, like Facebook and Tweeter, and help our economy? We need all the economic competitive edge that we can get around the world!

But no, we have these Pakis who only work during the work day, saying, There are cameras watching to see if we are surfing the net. I don't want to get into trouble. This kind of shit is going to keep us red-blooded Americans from technological developments and networking. After all, don't these fuckin' Pakis know that it's who you know and not what you know? They just don't play by the rules and make us all look bad!

But why don't we beat the be-Jesus out of these Pakis? Because we have been brain-washed in the zero-tolerance public school system and our claws, required to survive in the wild, have been plucked out of us. Yeah, so we let these nerdy Pakis walk all over us, and we let them dictate the terms on our own soil. God bless America! I say. We must guard our nation against foreign invasion. And this is the worse kind of invasion! These Pakis are killing American culture! What makes us Americans.

And Obamacare and the zero tolerance have made us into zoo animals. I just want to put a shut out to those red-blooded Americans who practiced their God-given right to bully a nerd in high school. Hey, you strengthened nerds through your bullying, so when they grew up with their MIT education, they were tough and were able to compete in the dog-eat-dog world. In other words, the bullying of nerds is an essential component for the nerds to lead America into the next century. It's like the sergeant in the boot camp. He calls you fuckin' worm, not because he hates you. He wants you to be a strong soldier. Can you imagine if there were zero tolerance in the Army? Shit! Saddam would have had all our boys bend over and sodomized like in some Catholic church in Wisconsin, when there is no mass in session.

See, why were these boys so easily sodomized? Well, I blame it on zero tolerance. Zero tolerance has weakened our boys in terms of their mental power and strength of the will. So, some fuckin' Democrat priest says to him, Bend over and take off your trousers, he's like, Okay. Yeah, I blame zero tolerance and taking away the toughness for this. Boys should be allowed to have roughness and have fights. In a controlled setting, this is a good thing. This is natural. If you have boys with pent up fighting instincts and bullying instincts, at some point, they will explode and then they will not know what to do. They will get some Glock pistol and start killing dozens of people. Pendulum swings from one extreme to the next. Let the boys be boys and duke it out through fist fighting, then you will decrease gun violence in schools. I blame the faggot Democrats for the weakening America and the weakening of American boys. And you see the consequences. You have a nation of faggots who are itching to bend over for some decrepit, impotent priest, who is confused by all the Political Correctness in the world. See what fucked up America? The faggot Democrats.

But don't tell people that I said all this because faggot Democrat-fueled America is still holding onto power. Eventually, everyone will realize what the problem was, but we still have a ways to go before hitting the bottom. And before we hit the bottom, people are not really going to pay attention, unfortunately.

But, yeah, sometimes what you least expect happens.

Chapter 8

But things happening the way you least expect it is not always a bad thing. Here, I was in Egypt, where one of the most beautiful women in human history, named Cleopatra, had lived. Here is the land of the Pharaohs. Here is the land of the Ten Plagues and the Exodus. Here are the exotic pyramids and the tombs of the Pharaohs. And in this land of surprises, something so unexpected has happened.

I was falling for Hadas, hard. I wasn't sure, still, if it was lust or love. But something was happening, and it was happening fast. It is shocking on one level because it happened so smoothly, like it was meant to be. I did not want to think about whether I was the rebound guy. I did not want to think about how she was using me to get back at her ex-boyfriend in some twisted way. I did not want to think about how I was being used for Hadas' temporary pleasure. A vacation fling.

I did not want to reduce what I was to anything smaller than the fairytale. I wanted this to be a fairytale romance. Prince meets a princess, falls in love, marries, and lives happily, ever after. I wanted to live in a fairytale for once in my life.

As my hand inched down Hadas' abdomen, she did not say much. She just kept her eyes closed. I wondered if she had fallen asleep. She just lay there with her eyes closed. Should I call out her name? What if she says, Yes, and opens her eyes? What will I say? It was, after all, an awkward moment. She was half-naked, and my hand was inching toward her most private spot.

Despite the feeling of being in the space that all the excitement and nervous anticipating created, I instinctively knew that this was not the moment to call out her name. I guess it's a biological thing. It's like knowing when to go to the bathroom, because nature is calling. At this time, nature was actually warning, like when you get a sick feeling in your stomach because you feel something bad will happen. More than not, something bad does happen.

As my hand inched down Hadas' undulating abdomen, I wondered how I came to be there at this moment, doing this. I felt like I was outside of my body, looking at myself. It felt surreal. It felt strange.

Slowly, my hand inched closer and closer toward her pink shorts. It was like bright white light that keeps attracting bugs to their death. It might bring death, but the bugs fly into it any way. I was wondering if this pull her pink shorts had on my hand was something that was like the bright white light that kills. Still, I could not stop. I allowed my hand to inch closer and closer toward the pink shorts.

I wondered what Hadas was thinking. She did not say anything. And she had her eyes closed. What kind of thoughts were going through her head?

My hand inched closer and closer toward the pink shorts. And tips of my fingers began to touch the pink shorts. It was a thin cotton-like material that my fingers brushed. And I no longer felt the wetness of my sweat or the undulation of her naked abdomen. Soon, my palms were on her pink shorts as well. I wondered what area my hands were covering. I wondered what color her hair down there was. It was kind of difficult to tell what her real hair color was. She could have colored her hair dirty-blonde, like some Israelis like to do. She looked attractive in her dirty-blonde hair and light white skin with freckles. Her eyes were bluish green. Maybe she was a natural blonde, and that hair color permeated through her body. I moved my fingers from side to side to see if I could feel some of the hair matter underneath the pink cotton. I felt a bit ridiculous, because I knew it was rationally impossible to feel the thin layer of hair underneath the cotton.

What surprised me, however, was that I did not feel the divide that characterizes women. I wondered why it was. Maybe the cotton-like substance was too rigid or too thick. I wondered if I could locate the schism. As my hand rested vertically on top of where there should be the divide, I felt the need to be more aggressive in the search for the opening. Thus, I lifted my hand about an inch off of her pink shorts and then started to trace with my index finger a vertical contour from the middle ground between her slightly quivering thighs in the direction of her undulating abdomen. My pinky finger touched her right thigh and my thumb brushed against her left thigh.

The first trace produced no fruitful result. I could not feel the divide. Confused and being a little impatient, I pushed my hand deeper into the empty space between her thighs and tried to trace the opening with the index finger. The second time around my index finger moved more quickly and exerted greater pressure against the pink shorts. Maybe I went too quickly through, because I could not distinguish the divide. I looked at her face in confusion, and I noticed her lips had parted. Her mouth was slightly open, and I could see that she was breathing more deeply. Her head had moved, and it was moving slightly from side to side. And I could see her hair moving around. This confirmed that she was not asleep.

Three times a charm. Thus, I reached with my hand toward the empty space between her thighs. I thought her thighs had moved a bit more apart, but I was not sure. It was a bit difficult to brush her right thigh with my pinky finger and her left thigh with my thumb at the same time. This time, the contour drawing of the pink shorts yielded a different experience. My index finger began to sink into a chasm. Even as I drew a line down the middle of her lower body, my index finger sank deeper and deeper. In fact, it felt like my index finger was plunging in. I could feel a profusion of liquid substance through the pink shorts. My index finger began to swim inside a newly created swimming pool. And I heard some squeaky noise coming out of Hadas, and I noticed Hadas' head moving with greater agitation. I began to make a more ovular shape inside the newly created swimming pool of her body. My index finger swam laps that were fast, such as a fast stroke. And then, there was an alteration of a slower backstroke. And the pink shorts felt wet from the natural juices of Hadas' oasis.

I felt the dryness of my mouth and longed to drink from the well-spring of her life. Life-giving waters produced deep within her body's core that was now bubbling up to the surface. Now, I only felt the wetness, and my finger was plunged in her body. As I relaxed my finger, it felt enwrapped by her body's core in the midst of her slightly moving hips. I wanted to taste the well-spring of her body, but there was a cover on the well. But my fingers felt the wetness, and I wanted to smell the aroma of the oasis of her body. I raised my finger up to my face, and I was slightly taken aback by the sudden relaxation of her body. Her wreathing has given away to a type of abandoned relaxation, allowing all of her body to relax.

She still had her eyes closed. Maybe, she too feared how I would look. How I would look at her. I wondered if she felt a sense of guilt at all. Or shame. Or was it just pleasure? Ironically, I know that guilt itself can feel like pleasure. The sense of going beyond what one should sometimes creates excitement of its own. And this excitement can become a snare that entraps. It can confine an individual to a prison of guilt, taken for pleasure. After all, there is the saying that curiosity killed the cat. The curiosity most likely referred to the curiosity laden with guilt. It is probably curiosity that one should not be curious about, at least, not yet.

I wondered where Hadas was in life. Then, I realized that I did not really know Hadas. Besides the fact that her boyfriend had cheated on her, I did not know much. Besides the fact that they broke up after the infidelity, I did not know much about Hadas. I did not know Hadas at all. Here I was with a stranger, and I did not know or know any background information to know what was going through her mind. She was a complete stranger to me, and here I was having access to her most private and intimate part of her physical being.

I wondered if I had the right. Did I have this right to her body? Was I taking advantage of her in any way? Should I not be doing this? What gave me the right to her most private parts? Somehow, I felt guilty about having this access. And I hesitated for a moment because I was overwhelmed by this privilege. How did I earn this privilege? Or was this right granted to me out of unmerited favor? She chose to grant me access, not based on anything I did to earn it, but simply because she wanted to. I did not know why I had this right, and this curiosity created hesitation.

I felt her body writhing underneath my finger and felt like my finger was like the finger on the ceiling of the Sistine Chapel in Rome – I am referring, of course, to the painting depicting creation. Somehow, my finger was creating something, as if out of nothing. *Creatio ex nihilo.* I felt a taste of what it felt like to be God. I felt simply divine. I felt like I was causing this woman's body to do things that she herself could not control. Her body was moving at my finger's touch, and I felt like the Creator. As she writhed, she began to moan in pleasure. I looked up at her face, and it looked like it was in a state of ecstasy. She was gasping for air like she was taking the most thrilling ride of her life. I wondered what it felt like to feel that way. What kind of sensations were going through her mind? As I gazed upon her and tried to empathize with her, I could not help but experience heated elevation of excitement. I felt my own body convulse with pleasure sensation and participated partially in her pleasure. And I could not control the excitement of my body, which seemed to have been seized strangely by this excitement. And without my expecting it, and without my desiring it, my excited member released its full load. I felt the warmth of my male juices fill my pants and felt a pang of embarrassment.

I did not know what to say to Hadas. I felt embarrassed. And I did not want to explain the situation. Suddenly, a cloud of fatigue descended upon my eyes, and I felt my eye lids shut. This, obviously, was convenient, and I gave in to my burden. Fatigue conquered my body the way the new husband conquered the body of his virginal bride, who had made every effort within her power to wait for the wedding night and had no strength or desire to resist. I opened my body fully to fatigue, and the fatigue did to my body what it willed. Within seconds, I feel asleep.

Chapter 9

I did not have any dreams. When I woke up, it felt like I had slept for one second. But obviously, it was not true, since I could hear all kinds of voices outside. It was clearly late morning. And since I felt refreshed, I knew that I had slept for a while. I felt a sense of pleasure at having had such a sweet sleep.

Then, I remembered. And whatever smile I might have had on my face, I am sure, quickly ran away from my face. I looked for Hadas. She was no longer attached to my finger. In fact, I did not see her body at all on the bed. I felt a pang of shock hit my head, and I felt a sudden headache. Where was she?

I looked around the room, and I saw her lying on the floor in a fetal position, apparently still asleep. I wondered why Hadas was lying on the floor. It was really odd. Did she fall off the bed? If she fell off the bed, then she should be near the bed. Like at the foot of the bed. But she wasn't. Why wasn't she there, right by the leg of the bed? Why was she all the way over there near the corner? How did she get there?

It was almost as if she had crawled over to the corner of the room and decided to take a fetal position and lie there. But that sounded odd. Why would anybody want to do that? Hadas is a normal person, and is so confident about herself. She is certainly not a weirdo or anything.

So, what was going on? Why was Hadas curled up in the corner of the room, all the way away from the bed, in a fetal position? I looked around the room, and I could see that in terms of geometry, she was at a spot that was physically the furthest away from where I was in the room. Was that intentional? Of course, it could not be intentional. I tried to picture in my mind Hadas getting up and looking around the room in the middle of the night and then picking a spot that was furthest away from me. Then, I tried to imagine her walking over there and then lying down. Then, I tried to picture her intentionally rolling herself in a fetal position. Nah! That couldn't be. Why would she do such a thing?

Maybe she sleepwalked. I have heard of stories of people sleepwalking middle of the night. In some cases, they have absolutely no memory of having sleepwalked. But they actually walk from one place to another. I guess there was only one way to find out. When Hadas wakes up, I could ask her if it is in her habit to sleepwalk. You can't blame someone for a medical condition, can you?

She lay there in the fetal position, and I noticed her body moving slightly as if she was breathing heavily. Her body did not have anything on it except for what was on her body when I fell asleep. I felt bad that she probably felt cold. The room was not cold. It is Egypt, after all. But I figured that it was a bit cold. Maybe that was why her body was moving like that. Maybe it was not breathing. Maybe it was her shivering. Ah, the poor girl! Shivering from cold.

I took the thin blanket and walked over to her and put it on her body. I saw her body stiffen. At least, that's what I thought I saw. I called out her name.

"Hadas?" No answer.

"Hadas?" I called out a second time.

I figured that she was tired from the long bus ride, and she was recuperating from the tiresome ride. I figured that girls need more beautiful sleep than guys. After all, girls' bodies are weaker. Hadas had been to the army, so maybe her body was tougher than mine. But I guess an army chick may not necessarily be stronger than a non-army guy. I wasn't a doctor or anything, so I could not offer any professional opinion on the issue. But I figured that this was logical.

I decided to let my curled up cat of a person sleep a little longer and went to the shower. The water was powerful and strong and hot. It felt good to take a hot shower in the morning. I thought about all the fun things Hadas and I were going to do together that day, and I felt a pang of happiness enter my heart. I felt lucky to be in Egypt with a cute chick to see Egypt. I wondered if she felt the same.

When I came out of the shower and opened the bathroom door, Hadas entered the bathroom. She was looking down at the floor as she walked, so I could not make out her face. I guess she was very tired. Sometimes, I feel groggy in the morning and don't feel like talking to anyone. I figured that was the mood Hadas was in.

I tried to cheer Hadas up. "Hadas, you are going to feel better after the shower. It feels so good!"

I heard a big bang as the bathroom door shut behind me.

"Geez," I said to myself, but also out loud. It was really loud, and it scared the bejesus out of me. Morning people don't always know their strength.

Hadas was in the shower for an awfully long time. I could feel my stomach crying out for food. "Feed me! Feed me!"

I felt bad for my stomach. The baby's gotta eat! It's crying out for food for God's sake! Why can't this woman hurry up?

Who takes a one-hour shower in the morning? For God's sake! I was getting a bit annoyed. I guess my hungry stomach was playing the instigator. How dare she take one hour shower? Now, I was mad at her. I gave her a pass on the rude shutting of the door. Hey, anyone can make a mistake. But now this? Is she for real? Was she going to tell me honestly that she did not notice time? That as her body became a raisin underneath all that water, she did not notice? For God's sake! We were in the desert! All the water she was consuming could be saving lives. Because of her one-hour plus shower, maybe a few people were going to die of thirst. Doesn't she have a heart? The poor water-deprived people of Egypt were just outside the window of our hotel. And she was going to heartlessly send them to dehydration and death from thirst. For what? For a one-hour-long shower? What vanity!

I was fully resolved to tell her all this when she walked out of the shower. I waited for the water to stop. It did not. It was now technically one hour fifteen minutes since the shower started running. Was the water still hot? Maybe she was standing under cold water? I remembered her shivering in the corner. Maybe she was going to catch a cold. Maybe, I could go in and rescue her. Maybe she fell asleep in the shower and was lying there under the cold water in the fetal position. Yes, the exact fetal position that I saw her in this morning when I woke up. That would not be cool. I began to worry about her.

"Hadas, are you okay in there?" I asked.

There was a moment of silence. But before I could call out her name for the second time, I heard a reply. "Mmm. Yeah, I am okay."

The voice sounded a little weak. Maybe she had caught cold already. Sleeping in a fetal position like that in the corner without any sheets on. What possessed her to do that?

She finally came out. I was about to give it to her. I was going to go on a prepared tirade about her having a long one-hour shower. But something stopped me. I looked at her eyes, and they looked puffy. Almost as if she had been crying.

"Hadas, what's wrong?" I was worried. "Did anything happen?"

She gave me a look. I did not know what it meant. I felt perplexed.

"Are you thinking about your ex-boyfriend?" I said. She looked away. "That jerk! What he did to you was horrendous!"

She murmured something, but I did not hear it, as she murmured at the end of my righteous indignation.

"Just forget about him," I said, feeling chivalrous.

"Yeah," Hadas said, not looking at me.

"By the way, why were you sleeping there curled up like a cat in the corner? Do you sleep walk?" I asked.

She shook her head and said, "Yeah, something like that."

I could not make her out. She felt a bit distant this morning. What was wrong with her? She was so friendly the day before.

Then, I realized. Is she mad at me because I went too far? Maybe it was too fast, too far. After all I had my finger stuck in her body. It felt a bit awkward as I remembered the night before. I thought she was enjoying it at the moment. But maybe she did not? Maybe in the morning she thought about it and was mad that I took advantage of her.

Did I take advantage of her? I tried to retrace the steps of the previous night. It did not feel like I had taken advantage of her. I thought she was sending me positive signals. But maybe I misread them? Maybe she wasn't sending positive signals, and I just assumed that she was sending positive signals, when in fact she was not sending any signals. Or maybe negative signals. I tried to freeze moments in time and analyze them. I don't know. But I can't remember any time in the previous night that would be construed as taking advantage without consent. Maybe Israeli culture is different?

After all, that Wiki Leaks guy was being extradited to Sweden because couple Swedish girls were saying that he raped them. One girl claimed that he had vaginal intercourse with her while she was asleep, and that constituted rape because she did not give consent at the particular time. The Wiki Leaks founder contended that it was not rape, because she had consented to a vaginal intercourse earlier that night, and she consented to his staying over. Thus, in a sense, since it was the same night and the consent was given earlier, the whole night would be seen as consensual. All this legal stuff is a bit confusing. But that Wiki Leaks guy is in deep shit because he did not understand Swedish Law. I don't think in America, a girl can claim rape using the same arguments. But then, what do I know? Maybe they can? I am no lawyer. And I bet half the lawyers would be befuddled at that one. I guess it would be one for the US Supreme Court to decide. But can you imagine? It's a pretty embarrassing case for the US Supreme Court to deliberate on. Can you imagine all the late night comedian jokes?

"Did you hear about that new US Supreme Court case? Clearance Thomas looked mighty nervous on that chair."

"You sure it was nervousness? Maybe he was excited, thinking about his Anita Hill days."

Ha, ha, ha. The whole nation laughs.

Poor, Clearance Thomas. Uncle Tom, many blacks call him, because he is a Republican and black. Peeping Tom, the feminists call him, because of Anita Hill. Now, he may be called, "Tom, Tom," as people shake their heads.

But this world is becoming wacky for guys and gals and relationships. You need like a handbook to understand what's going on, and this has to be the international, cultural sensitivity edition.

Granted, having vaginal intercourse with a woman when she is asleep doesn't seem like a gentlemanly thing to do. But would it be considered rape if she gave consent like one hour before and allowed you to stay the night in her bed, both of you naked? And she did not say before falling asleep. Please, don't put your thingy in any of my orifices when I am asleep. So, she cannot say that she prohibited him from love making in any format.

Let's look at it from another angle. If a girl that you had sex with is sucking on your penis while you are sleeping, then is she raping you? Obviously, there is probably not a single guy who would object to that action by a girl that he fancies. And all guys are dogs, who want it as much as he can get it, so maybe the illustration is not fair. But still there is some correlative insight here, I think.

It is very difficult to cry rape when you had created that kind of a scenario. I am not saying that you can't claim rape, if you said, "Don't" to the second time, maybe because you had a fight, and he forced himself upon you after your objection. But the objection was registered. But if you had not uttered the objection before you or he fell asleep. And there was no objection registered during the act, can you claim rape? I would think that it would be difficult to argue that point.

Anyhow, I digress.

Why is Hadas in such a bad mood? Maybe it's that time of the month? I heard that women get all argumentative when they are about to have their period. Maybe that's what it is. Why are they cranky? Do they have muscle spasms or something? I guess I would get cranky if I have a spasm in my groin the way I have on in my leg. But not being a woman, it is hard to picture what PMS is like. Maybe I should Google it and become more informed. Certainly, not until this Egypt trip is done and over with. I figure that we'll be back to Israel before her next month's attack, so I could push it off for a month. And we won't be together like this 24-7 when we are back in Israel, so I shouldn't feel the full brunt of her PMS anger. So, fuck it! I just need to grit and bear it for today. Does PMS last for more than a day? Hope not.

"So, ready to head on out?" I said, trying to put on a positive spirit.

"Yeah," Hadas said slowly. I thought I detected her coldness eroding.

"Maybe, we'll do what you want," I said. "We can go see an Egyptian protest."

"Maybe, another time," Hadas said. "I don't feel like doing it, today."

"But you seemed so enthusiastic, yesterday, about it," I said, puzzled.

"Let do something else," Hadas said curtly.

"Okay," I said. "Why don't we go see the pyramids?"

"Sounds good," Hadas said.

I thought she was making an effort, so I began to breathe a sigh of relief.

We had our complimentary breakfast at the hotel, which was basically a couple toasts with jams. We felt sufficiently filled that we felt ready for the pyramids.

"We'll have more food when we get to the pyramids," I said.

"Sounds good," Hadas said.

"We'll have food for the gods," I said, trying to make a joke. "The foods that the great Pharaohs ate."

"Just don't sell me to someone else for 100 camels," Hadas said.

"Ha, ha," I said. "You are so funny."

Hadas smiled. She was warming up!

I said, "Of course, not for 100 camels." Then, I paused for a few seconds. "But for 200 camels, I might be persuaded."

"Then, you would just become a pimp!" Hadas responded.

"No," I said. "A pimp sells his woman to many men for a timeslot share."

Hadas looked at me with a curious look.

"I would be more like a matchmaker," I said. "Matchmaker, matchmaker, make me a match!" I tried to sing a tune from the musical, "The Fiddler on the Roof."

"Always the best man and never the groom!" Hadas said, shaking her head. I thought I detected a bit of bitterness in her tone.

"You mean," I said. "Always the bridesmaid and never the bride! I think that's actually the right saying."

"According to whom?" Hadas said contentiously.

"According to everyone," I said. "It's like a saying."

"Well," Hadas said. "I don't agree."

"Hadas," I said. "It's not about agreement. It's just a saying that everyone agrees with."

"Well," Hadas said. "Maybe everyone is wrong, and I am right."

"Okay," I said. "You are not going to take out your M-16 and start shooting me, are you?"

I tried levity, but it did not work. Hadas said with a cold tone, "Maybe, I will."

"You are not mad at me, are you?" I said, a bit alarmed.

"Why would I be mad at you?" Hadas said. "Is there any reason that I should be mad at you?"

Her glaring stare made me fumble my words. "Well, no," I said. "I hope not."

I felt like a dweeb. I hope not? What a stupid response! But the cat was out of the bag, and I could not call it back, so I just sat there in the taxi, waiting for some biting sarcastic comment to come back and totally humiliate me.

To my surprise, I heard nothing. I was literally about to cover my head, like when there are things falling all around you from the sky and you want to protect your head. And I heard nothing. Were my ears working right? Nothing? Really?

I opened one eye towards Hadas to see if she was preparing a full-frontal assault, and she was just taking her time before the big kill. But surprisingly, she was looking outside the window, apparently in some kind of thought.

"Of course, you should not be mad at me," I said.

She looked back with a smile on her face. "I know a reason why I should be mad at you."

There was a silence. There was a glare. And there was a more intense silence. And I felt my heart beating. Louder and louder. I looked at my watch. One minute had passed. Maybe it was not even one minute, since I don't have a digital watch nor a second hand on my watch. I was looking at the minute hand. Maybe the minute hand had not moved even a millimeter. I can't tell.

"You said you would sell me for 200 camels," Hadas said with that eureka look.

"No, I said, I would consider selling you for 200 camels," I said.

"It's the same thing," Hadas said.

"No, it isn't," I said. "Selling and considering selling are completely different."

"Semantics," Hadas said. "But both show that you are not that into me. You are willing to sell me."

"I am very much into you!" I said loudly. I noticed the taxi driver looking at me through his rearview mirror at that moment of confession. He smiled and shook his head.

I felt a bit embarrassed that I had made the comment so emphatically, so I shut up.

"If you were very much into me, then you would never sell me for even 1000 camels!" Hadas explained.

"You are assuming that I am an honorable man," I said, smiling and joking.

"Well, aren't you?" Hadas said.

"Do I look like an honorable man to you?" I said, smiling a bigger smile.

"So, you are saying that looks can be deceiving?" Hadas said.

"No, I am just asking a question," I said.

"How very Rabbinic of you to answer a question with a question!" Hadas said sarcastically.

"But, of course, that is the Jewish way," I said.

"But you are not Jewish!" Hadas said.

"Yeah, but," I said, trying to fish for words, "that does not mean that I cannot use the Jewish way!"

"You are full of it," Hadas said, shaking her head.

"Yeah, full of love for you," I said and smiled at her.

"You are such a smooth talker," Hadas said. "But will you deliver the goods when it's time."

"Yeah, baby," I said. "Thirty minutes for your or the pizza is free!"

"Huh?" Hadas said.

"It's an American thing," I said.

"What does it mean?" Hadas said, puzzled.

"In America, several pizza places try to lure customers by saying that their pizza will be free if they don't deliver it within 30 minutes of ordering it."

"But that is begging for car accidents and breaking of road speed laws," Hadas said.

"Yes, and I am sure many a pizza delivery boys became literally criminals and did real time because of it," I said. "But some pizza joints became successful businesses because of it. That's capitalism. Some win and some lose."

"Bah to your American capitalism!" Hadas said.

"Bah to your Israeli pizza!" I said in return.

"What do you mean?" Hadas said.

"Israeli pizza sucks," I said. "Tuna on pizza? What's up with that?"

Hadas said, "You know we are Jews, so we have to be kosher. When you mix beef with cheese, its not kosher."

"So, you are going to do the Satanic thing and mix tuna with your cheese pizza?" I asked. "There must be some cosmic law higher than Torah that prohibits that."

"What?" Hadas said. "It's delicious. You don't have that in the USA?"

"Maybe if you go to Brooklyn to a Hasidic neighborhood and find a kosher pizza place run by Hasidic Jews," I said. "But in a normal pizza place? Hell, no!"

"You should try it," Hadas said. "It's actually quite good."

"There are a few things that Americans do not do even under the gravest of tortures, like the Chinese water torture," I said. "That is eat pizza with tuna on it. It is simply anti-American. It's like betraying America to do that."

"What is Chinese water torture?" Hadas asked.

"That's when they tie you down and have a drop of water hit your forehead every few seconds," I explained. "After a few hours of that, each drop of water is supposed to feel like lead."

"How do you know?" Hadas asked. "Have you tried it?"

"No," I said. "I don't know where to get the Chinese water torture machine that will drop one drop in equal increments.

"But you believe what you hear?" Hadas said. "I bet it's not a torture at all. I bet the Chinese have never used this method."

"Okay, fine," I said. "When we go back to Israel, we'll Google it and find out."

"You Americans are like the handicapped who need the crutch called Google," Hadas said. "Google is your new God."

"Well, that's what Google tried to be," I said. "But sorry, Google. Apple pushed you out of the way!"

"Yeah," Hadas said, "I heard that Apple is the biggest company in the world."

"All thanks to iPhone, iPod, iPad," I said.

"The Holy Trinity of electronics," Hadas added.

"Don't let that Coptic Christian hear you blaspheme like that," I said and pointed to a person who looked like a Coptic Christian in the street.

"You sure he is Coptic?" Hadas said.

"He's wearing that Coptic cross on his chest," I said.

"No," Hadas said. "I think that it is a trinket he is selling."

"Well, you get my point," I said, irritated.

"No, I don't," Hadas said. "You ruined a great metaphor with one of your digressionary comments that is not related at all."

"I don't think digressionary is a word," I said.

"You see!" Hadas said. "I rest my case."

"You know what a Harvard professor said?" I asked.

"What?" Hadas said.

"It is in digressions that you discover something monumental," I said.

"That can't be true," Hadas said. "It's like saying that accidents are the cause for great discoveries."

"I guess it's stretching it, but you can argue that," I said.

"That doesn't make sense," Hadas said.

"Did you know that penicillin was discovered by accident?" I said.

"No," Hadas said.

"And penicillin saves millions of lives," I said.

"What does that make us?" Hadas said.

"Products of a big divine joke," I said.

"And you believe this?" Hadas asked seriously.

"Why should we have all the fun?" I said. "I am sure that God has a sense of humor and we are that."

"You are saying that God created us for amusement?"

"Yeah," I said. "Why not?"

"But that does not make sense," Hadas said.

"Of course, it makes sense," I said.

"It cheapens God," Hadas said.

"What do you care, Hadas," I said. "You don't even believe in God."

"See, another one of your digressions," Hadas said. But before I could interrupt her, she said, "I don't believe in God, but I am open to believing in him. After all, I am a Jew."

"What does that mean?"

Hadas looked at me and could not answer.

"See?" I said. "You don't even know what that means!"

"Well," Hadas said. "I am Jewish because my mother's Jewish."

"Really?" I said. "Are you really going to hold to that line?"

"That's like Talmudic rule for who is Jewish."

I objected, "But you yourself do not believe in the Jewish God."

"I don't believe in any God," Hadas said. "But I am not a Nazi about it. I am open to it, if I can be persuaded."

"Okay," I said. "I will persuade you that God has a sense of humor."

"So, you are not going to persuade me that there is a God?" Hadas said.

"Well, let's jump that step," I said, "and for the sake of argument assume that there is God. And if there is God, I would argue that he has a sense of humor."

"Okay, I will hear you out," Hadas said.

"God has humor because devout believers die of cancer after suffering for years and depleting family savings," I said.

"How does that show that God has a sense of humor?" Hadas asked. "It makes God look evil not humorous."

"I did not say that God has a sense of humor that benefits us," I said. "You may laugh when someone farts even though that person is embarrassed. You are having fun at his expense."

"Yeah," Hadas said, "but that is different."

"How is that different?" I asked. "It's not funny to the guy who just farted!"

"No," Hadas said. "The whole situation is funny. And it is not hurting anyone."

"How about when someone trips a nerd?" I said. "When the nerd falls in the cafeteria with all his food, most people will find that funny."

"Well, that's mean," Hadas said.

"Can you honestly tell me that you did not find such situations funny in high school?" I asked with a serious tone.

"Of course, not!" Hadas said. "I am not a monster."

"But you are a liar!" I said. "You are not being honest. You did not feel a bit of the smiles? At all?"

"Okay," Hadas said. "Maybe a little bit."

"Okay," I said. "You are no longer a liar, but you are a monster."

"Ha, ha," Hadas said with an ironic tone.

"Do you see my point?" I said. "What is not funny to the nerd is funny to you, even if he get a bruise in the process."

"And you are saying that God is like that?" Hadas said. "And this is going to persuade me to believe in a God?"

"No," I said. "If you remember, I am not trying to persuade you to believe in a God. I am merely trying to prove to you that God has a sense of humor."

"And you are saying that it is a monstrous sense of humor," I said.

"Call it what you want," I said. "What you consider painful or disastrous, God considers funny."

"But that's sick," Hadas said.

"Well, if you want," I said, "call it God's sick sense of humor. He's God and can do whatever he wants. Even have a sick sense of humor. Who's going to tell him not to. You? The US Military?"

"So, you are saying that God gives cancer to a devout believer just to have a laugh?" Hadas said.

"You know how many devout Hasidic Jews were killed in the Holocaust?" I said. "Why did he not stop it? After all, they worship him?"

"And you are saying that it is because God finds that funny?" Hadas said incredulously.

"Haven't you seen someone who had a pet cat cut a bit of the cat's ear off?" I aked.

"No," Hadas said. "You have sick friends."

"I am not saying that I have such friends, but I am trying to illustrate a point," I said.

"Well, use another example," Hadas said. "Leave the cute cats alone."

"Okay," I said. "Consider this. Have you ever seen a movie where someone who is devoted to a gangster or a bully becomes that bully's punching bag?"

Hadas looked at me puzzled.

"Why is it that some bullys bully their own followers?" I asked.

"Because they are bullies?" Hadas said with a "duh" expression on her face.

"Well, yes," I said. "But because they are amused by it."

"So, you are saying that God is a bully?" Hadas said.

"Do you doubt it?" I said. "Of course, he is a bully!"

"That's a bit harsh!" Hadas said.

"Who else would take your immortality away because you ate the forbidden fruit?" I said.

"Yeah, but that story is fiction," Hadas said.

"Let's assume that the story is real," I said. "Don't you think God is a bit of a bully for taking eternity away just because Adam and Eve ate some fruit? Isn't that like bully action?"

"Well," Hadas hesitated.

"Of course, it is!" I said. "God is a bully, who has a bully sense of humor. Let's face the facts."

"Okay," Hadas said with her eyes wide open.

"And let's go to the story of Noah," I said. "God is such a big bully that God tells poor Noah to built a big boat in the middle of nowhere, far from any body of water, like he is an idiot. Everyone in his neighborhood is like, 'There is that cookoo Noah, building a big ship middle of nowhere, instead of doing a normal job, like farming. And there is no water anywhere nearby!' So, God in his bully sense of humor tells his devout follower Noah to make himself look like an idiot for years and years and suffer humiliation for years and years. For what? Nothing. God just want to have a laugh. And then, what does this bully God do? He kills the whole world by flood. And as everyone drowns to death, Noah could feel a sick sense of pleasure of his God as he sees everyone die around him. And Noah was probably like 'Ha, ha, you are drowning to death! You deserve it, you assholes, for making fun of me for building this ark. Who has the last laugh?' See what a bully God is. God bullies Noah and forces him to suffer humiliation. By that time,

Noah is so twisted in the head, that Noah is jumping up and down and laughing at people who bullied him because God put him in that spot. Did God really have to kill everyone? Of course not! Why did he do it? He just wanted to have a laugh."

"I don't know," Hadas said.

"Do you have another explanation?" I asked.

"No, but I am sure I can come up with something better," Hadas said.

"What do you care about God's reputation?" I said. "You don't believe that he exists."

"But you do," Hadas said.

"Yes, I do," I said.

"Then, why do you want God to have such a bad reputation?" Hadas said.

"No," I said. "It about being honest about God. God is really this way, and this is the way God wants to be known. That is why God said, 'I am who I am.'"

"What? A jerk?" Hadas protested.

"Well, why not?" I said. "God has the right to be remembered in the way he wants to be remembered. Why should we deny God his right to be who he is? What right do we have to lie about God's identity?"

"Have you gone to a synagogue, lately?" Hadas said.

"You know, I am a Christian," I said.

"Well, then, to a church?" Hadas said.

"Yes, in Jerusalem," I said.

"And the priests would agree with you?" Hadas asked.

"If they are honest, then they have to," I said. "But there are a lot of phonies in the world, including phonies in the Vatican, phonies in bishop positions, phonies who teach theology, phonies who lie through their teeth about God's identity, ignoring God's own self-revelation. It's like they want to sanitize God for the 21st century Political Correctness culture. I say, it's time to be honest. Honest with God. Honest with ourselves."

161

"I bet those religious leaders will hate you," I said.

"Well, phonies will hate truth-sayers, won't they?" Hadas said.

"But you are not holy or anything," Hadas said.

"I don't claim to be holy," I said. "In fact, I claim to be sinner of sinners. That's why I need God."

"I don't know," Hadas said. "It sounds twisted."

"Well, I am just repeating what's in the religious text," I said. "Religious texts preserved for thousands of years don't lie. Phonies do."

"That's deep," Hadas said, like she wanted to close the chapter on the conversation.

"Very serious conversation," the taxi driver jumped in.

He took both of us by surprise. I said, "So, what do you think?"

"I think this white Christian boy has a point," the taxi driver said.

Hadas just shook her head.

"Well, we are here," the taxi driver said. "Try to enjoy the pyramids."

"Thank you," we both said and left the taxi.

Chapter 10

The pyramids looked magnificent. It certainly looked better the more I saw them.

"Wow," Hadas said. "It's really amazing."

"Isn't it?"

"Yeah, but I am hungry," Hadas said.

"Me, too," I said. "The pyramids have been there for thousands of years, so I am sure they can wait for us. Let's grab something to eat."

As we walked to a nearby restaurant, I noticed someone that I knew.

"Dodi?" I said.

Dodi looked very surprised.

"Dodi, what are you doing here?" I said in surprise.

"I guess," Dodi caught himself, "I guess I am doing what you are doing."

"And that is?" I asked.

"Taking in the sights," Dodi said.

"But you never said anything about that?" I said. "What's up with that?"

"Well," Dodi said. "I don't have to tell you everything, do I?"

A woman who was a bit far off came towards us when she heard the commotion. I don't really know what she was doing back there. But another surprise awaited me.

"Hagit?" I said, flabbergasted.

Hagit looked at me, but it did not seem like she looked embarrassed at all.

"What are you doing here, Hagit?" I asked. "Don't you have the military?"

Hagit and Dodi looked at each other and smiled. What was that?

"Do you know each other?" I said.

They looked at me, trying to suppress the smiles.

"Did you know each other before that night?" I said as I felt some uneasy anger arise.

They just looked at me.

"Yeah, you did," I said. "Didn't you?"

Dodi nodded.

"So, are you even in the army?" I asked Hagit.

Hagit just looked at me. "Sorry, mate," Dodi said. "I am afraid not."

"So, you played a little game at my expense?" I demanded.

"Pete, be a good sport," Dodi said.

"And now, you two have followed me here to poke fun of me more?" I said.

"Yeah," Dodi said. "You can say that." And Dodi started to laugh.

I felt a rush of anger flood, and I saw red. I just rushed Dodi and pushed him down to the ground. I heard a big thump as he fell and I fell on top of him.

"Come on, Pete," Dodi said. "You don't want to do this. I can kick your butt with my hands tied behind my back."

"No, you can't," I tried to pin Dodi down. I had forgotten that Dodi had military training, and he was good at fighting, even before he joined the military. And he was a big guy.

I still tried to push Dodi down against the ground. Dodi lost patience and did one of his maneuvers and flipped me over, right there in the Egyptian street. I was slammed against the hard dirt floor and felt pain all over. I could taste blood in my mouth.

"You shouldn't mess with Dodi," Hagit said.

Oh, great. The Israeli chick I thought was my crowning achievement and a potential love of my life was mocking me like I was her nephew or something. It was humiliating!

"That's not cool," Hadas came to my rescue. Hadas bent down and brushed my face with her fingers. "Are you okay, Pete?"

"I think so," I told Hadas. "Oh, you poor thing, you look like you need tender loving care."

I don't know why, but I felt a streak of tear dropping from my eyes onto my cheeks. I guess it might have been the tenderness that Hadas showed me when I was in pain. She could be so motherly. Who could have imagined that she had it in her?

Maybe it was the fact that I felt betrayed like Jesus did with Judas. This was Dodi, my Israeli best friend. He had set me up. I felt like I was the idiot invited to the dinner for idiots, in which a bunch of executives of a company bring whom they figure to be an idiot, just to poke fun of them. What rich people do for fun! It just does not make sense to ordinary folk. But they do weird things like that. No wonder there are revolutions, like the French Revolution and the American Revolution and the Bolshevik Revolution. Probably the weirdness of the rich folk has more to do with instigating the revolt than the oppression itself. What is Catharine the Great of Russia known for, for God's sake? See, what I mean? Weird stuff!

I looked at Hadas, and I noticed Hadas throwing an evil look at my friends. It's strange how a total stranger that you just met a few days ago can be a better friend to you than someone whom you consider to be your best friend. I wonder if it was jealousy that played a role in Dodi's betrayal of me.

One reason theologians point to for the cause-effect of why Judas betrayed Jesus Christ is that Jesus Christ allowed a woman to pour oil on his feet. The value of the oil was more than one month's salary. A beautiful woman pouring expensive oil like that could make anyone jealous. And it made Judas jealous enough to betray Jesus Christ.

Not only that, Judas did not like Jesus Christ's attitude towards the poor, some claim. When Judas rebuked the woman for wasting precious oil on Jesus' feet that could have been sold to help the poor, Jesus Christ rebuked Judas and said that the poor will always be there, but Jesus Christ would not be. In a sense, Jesus Christ was saying, "Screw the poor! I am going to get some!" Jesus Christ wanted the expensive stuff on his person, even if it meant that some poor people would have to starve to death for it.

Who said that Jesus Christ is on the side of the poor? Obviously, these people did not read their New Testament carefully. Some Democrats are trying to make Jesus Christ out to be some liberal Democrat. They try to argue that Jesus Christ would support Obama's healthcare reform. There is no bigger mount of cow manure than that. Jesus Christ would have opposed Obama's healthcare reform, because at no time in his ministry did Jesus Christ tried to help the poor get out of their poverty. In other words, even though Jesus Christ had three years of ministry, there is not even one account in any place in the New Testament where Jesus Christ helped a poor family have an extra meal.

No, Jesus Christ would not have helped out in the soup kitchen. That's not his thing. Today's American Christians do not read their New Testament, so they think that Jesus Christ cared about bringing the poor out of poverty. That's nowhere close to the truth. Christ wanted the poor to remain poor. Christ wanted the poor to die of hunger. There is not even one recorded event where Christ saved a person from dying of hunger. And, yes, just like today, there were beggars back then. But Jesus Christ does not help a single one.

So, where do today's Christians get their "Help the Poor" ethics? Certainly, not from Jesus Christ! Jesus Christ did jack shit for the poor, and the New Testament is the documentary evidence that proves it. Any clergyman who says that Jesus Christ cared about saving the poor from their financial difficulties is a big-fat liar! Show me from the Bible, where Jesus Christ rescues a poor person from his poverty.

What's the problem with today's American Christians is that they have lost their way. They assume that helping the poor pleases God. And the New Testament shows that they assume wrong. Is it any wonder why God is causing America to suffer economic collapse? Because America's Christians are focused on wrong things, like helping the poor. The primary goal of the New Testament is to force people to accept the divinity of Jesus Christ. To hell with the poor! That is the message of the Christian Gospel. But there are too many phonies in America's evangelical circles, and they have twisted the Gospel mostly use church resources to help the poor. They have lost their way. They have lost their truth.

Helping the poor was the stumbling block that caused Judas Iscariot to betray Jesus Christ. Helping the poor can be evil. It is better to build an expensive church for Jesus Christ than feed the poor. That is the Christian Gospel. And we know this because Christ wanted expensive oil on his feet rather than feeding the poor. Today's so-called Christians should read the Bible more.

Jesus Christ would hate Obama's healthcare reform, and he would condemn it with a passion, just as he condemned Judas Iscariot. God's ways are not man's ways, and man's ways are not God's ways. To assume what humans consider to be good is what God considers to be good is assuming too much. And that's the mistake Judas Iscariot made. And that is the mistake so many phonies who call themselves Christians make in the United States, today. Often, people view Jesus through their personal lens. I guess that the human tendency is to view things from their personal lens.

Hadas' tenderness struck a cord with me because it was tenderness directed at me, personally. I guess that we all view the world through the personal lens. Everyone is biased toward himself or herself. You can't avoid that. One cannot feel another's pain, no matter how much one tries. The pain felt by a mother who suffers breast cancer and has to get rid of one of her breasts is the pain that only she herself can understand. No matter how much her family members love her, they cannot understand that pain. Not really.

And that is similar with joy. When a person is admitted to Harvard University and experiences an elated joy, his parents cannot feel that even if they try very hard. They may be happy for their son, but they can never understand the sensation that he is feeling as he reads his acceptance letter.

All experience is personal. In a sense, therefore, everyone is an island. One experiences only what one experiences. One can really only understand what one experiences. As the other, one cannot understand. One stands as one.

The problem with the United States of America and especially with the Democrats is that they think that they understand. As Bill Clinton lied through his teeth, "I feel your pain," stupid Americans believed him. They still believe him. And that is why Bill Clinton is one of the most popular presidents. Americans stupidly want to be understood, so they fool themselves into thinking that the other can understand. The other can't, because the other is not you.

I tell you what else Bill Clinton felt. Yeah, the I-did-not-have-sex-with-that-woman president, whose semen was on the dress of that Jewess Monika Lewinsky. She's kind of like Esther who brought a leader down, but unlike Esther, she was not an upright woman.

168

Hadas' tenderness towards me made me feel more tenderness towards her. I guess love is reciprocal. What do I mean? Because I know that Hadas is acting in a loving way towards me, I feel inspired to love her. In a sense, love is selfish. Would I love Hadas, if I knew that she did not love me? Probably not. There has to be something there. I need to be convinced in my own mind, however twisted it may be, that she loves me, for me to love her and continue to love her.

Marriage ends in divorce, not because the marriage partner stops loving him from the beginning. But for some reason, she puts it in her head that he no longer loves her. Being convinced that he no longer loves her, she stops loving him, out of the impetus from her rational mind or emotion. It is, in other words, a conscious choice to stop loving him. It is after the marriage partner takes the conscious step to stop loving her husband, that her rational mind works to convince her that she is no longer in love. Everything he does begins to look bad. She finds examples after examples to confirm why she no longer loves him. What was the cause to this effect? It is the rational deduction, however accurate or not, that her husband no longer loves her.

Maybe the impetus started because he started working late and forgot to call. Maybe it is because he snapped at her more than usual during stressful periods. It could be the glance that her husband throws her acquaintance, which she interprets as the kind of glance that her husband used to throw her and throw only at her, frequently. It is possible that she is misreading the situation. It could be that her husband is faking nicety for his wife's own sake, since she is your acquaintance or business partner. But that does not mean that the marriage partner could not misread the events and your intention.

All divorce can be avoided. Why? Because when two people married, they believed that they loved one another. Even if they can effectively maintain this mirage, the marriage can last until their death. But the problem is that with habit, people become careless. Often, it is comfort that is misinterpreted as falling out of love. For example, when you first date a girl, you would never fart in front of her. At least, for most guys. But after you have been together with her for about a year, at least 30% of the guys would have no problem farting right in front of his girlfriend or wife. Should this be evidence for falling out of love?

Of course, not! Since he farts when he is alone because he is comfortable with himself, he will fart in front of his brother because he is familiar. Same with the parents. In fact, the wife should be flattered that her husband feels comfortable enough to fart in front of her. But she may not read it that way. She may read it as carelessness or rudeness that is opposite of love. She may think that this is the evidence that her husband no longer loves her or no longer loves her the way he did before. This inception of doubt may ultimately end in divorce. Such doubt can have a domino effect on one's mind, you see. And all interpretation can be colored by this singular thesis.

But of course, divorce can be prevented, if such doubt is crushed. But it requires the bondage of the will. Binding of runaway logic that is misguided.

Well, you can say that it may be actually that the husband no longer loves the wife. Image is everything, as the saying goes. Let's take a case of a husband cheating on his wife. Why would he do that if he loves his wife? But assuming that the cheating husband no longer loves his wife may be misguided. Consider this possibility. The husband cheated on his wife because guys can be dogs. Guys want to hump anything that moves. It is not that he no longer loves his wife. It is just that he is a dog. So, infidelity cannot be seen as a proof that the husband no longer loves his wife. Man can hump 10 different women and truly love his wife. But the wife may not want to consider that possibility because she is in pain because her husband's infidelity strikes as her pride, her self-perception, her self-worth, and preconceived rational conclusion that a husband who loves will not cheat. But humans make mistakes. Humans fail. That's what makes humans, well, humans.

So, even in the case of infidelity, husband cannot be blamed for not loving his wife. Let's see this from another angle. Sometimes, men feel a need to cheat to establish their masculinity or sense of control. Why does he do this? Maybe, because his wife refuses to have sex with him. Does it justify infidelity? No. But we are merely trying to understand the cause-and-effect relationship.

Thus, when a wife withholds sex, she has to take some blame for her husband's infidelity. After saying more than 3 nights in a row that she has a headache and cannot have sex, if her husband has sex with another woman, then, obviously the wife has to take some of the blame for the infidelity. Does she really have a headache? As a wife, she should be selfless and be willing just to lie there while her husband pleasures himself with her body. It's give and take. You can't be selfish and deny your husband his sexual pleasure just because you have a headache. This goes against the Bible.

In fact, the Bible understands human nature. Bible says that husband and wife are required to put out when the other want sex. Yes, it's right there in print. So, if you don't put out when your marriage partner wants some, then you are sinning against God because Bible requires you to put out. Sin is disobedience to God. When God says put out for your husband, then you put out for your husband. None of this I-have-a-headache excuse! Obedience to God brings happiness, no?

Why are so many Americans divorced? Because they sin against God by not putting out when their marriage partner wants it. You are tired? Fine, go to sleep. What's wrong with your husband entering your body when you are asleep? Marriage means that your body no longer belongs to you. Your husband's body belongs to you, and your own body belongs to your husband. It would be wrong to deny him his pleasure. If you are tired, just sleep through it. But he should have his pleasure as it is his divine right as your husband.

The my-body argument does not work with God. It is because of sin of not putting out that God is punishing Americans with unhappiness resulting from divorce and alienation from children and other suffering related with divorce. If Christians followed the handbook, that is the Bible, then there should be no problems in marriage. Not putting out it sin, just as much as killing someone. Bible is God's Word, and God's rules for putting out must be followed.

America is one fucked up country. Christians think that feeding the poor is doing God's will when Jesus never ever fed the poor for the reason that they are poor. Fucked up Christians and fucked up churches with their fucked up notions of the poor and how Christ fits into that.

America is really fucked up. They get divorced and say it's okay, when Jesus Christ specifically said in the New Testament that divorce is wrong. For God's sake, Jesus Christ himself explicitly forbade divorce! How can someone say that she is a follower of Jesus Christ and get a divorce? What a liar! What a hypocrite! In the sight of Christ, divorce is more evil that killing someone. But American Christians are fucked up and they ignore the words of Christ. No wonder why God fucks up their lives. They fuck with God, and God fucks with them. Just don't fuck with God, and you will be okay. Yes, America is a fucked up country. And American Christians are fucked up. Really fucked up!

At least the Vatican is sticking by the Biblical position on divorce. You know, we may be sinners, but we have to acknowledge God's Word as it is. It's just fucked up to twist everything around the way many liberal Christians in America do to justify their actions. God of the Bible has given a revelation for a reason!

I looked at Hadas and her tenderness, and felt the tenderness that Jesus Christ had for his followers. Jesus Christ might have treated Jewish leaders with hatred, calling them hypocrites and brood of vipers, but Jesus Christ surely loved his disciples. Even when Jesus Christ hung from the cross, he cared about his mother, who was also his follower. When I looked at the tenderness of Hadas, I felt like I might have caught a glimpse of the tenderness that Jesus Christ showed to his mother, and I was deeply touched.

Hadas said some rapid things in Hebrew and drove Dodi and Hagit away. It happened so fast, that I had no time to respond. Hadas took out some tissues and wiped blood away from my mouth, as soon as she saw that Dodi and Hagit had left. And then, we went to a nearby restaurant for some grub. I did not feel much like eating because I tasted blood in my mouth. I don't think any teeth were broken. Some areas inside my mouth seemed to have been cut, along with my lips.

Although I did not feel like eating on one level, I felt the hunger deeply on another level. Thus, I caved in to my hunger and had some food. It was Arabic food that I was not familiar with. Hadas ordered them and told me that they were good. And they were quite good. It is good to be traveling with a knowledgeable person. It is really good to be traveling with someone who cares.

I did not talk too much during the meal. I felt like my relationship with Hadas had entered a different level. I felt closer to her and more attached to her. I never expected her to be my protector and shield. She was shorter than me and smaller. And when you look at her, she did not impress you as a Rottweiler. But that's what she was. At least, for me. And this surprise both fascinated me and intrigued me. She had become my savior, when I least expected it.

But I could not shake off the sense of embarrassment that was creeping in. She had stood up for me and defended me, when that is the role that I should have had. But the embarrassment soon dissipated, because I am not particular about such things. I don't mind a woman defending me. I don't mind a woman rescuing me.

Maybe I am different from other men in this. But I am not too sure I am that different. After all, Florence Nightingale gained fame and adoration of men all over the world, because she rescued men injured in the war. It might be different in context and extent, but surely Nightingale was a hero to those soldiers the way Hadas was to me, today. Surely, those men saw her as a savior, the way I saw Hadas.

Some men might have felt some embarrassment, but by in large, I don't think so. I have heard a female friend say that all men are babies. Men are taken care of by their mothers and then when they get married, they are taken care of by their wives. Thus, men live their whole existence being taken care of by women. And men who do not have that luxury often live like pigs in a pigsty.

Hadas and I walked toward the pyramid after our meal. Hadas kept throwing me a glance, as if she was checking in on a sick child. I wanted to tell her that I was feeling okay, but I couldn't because she did not ask the question. I tried to smile and reassure her, but for some reason words escaped me. I could not tell the usual jokes that I wanted to tell. In fact, my mind went completely blank. I tried to bring some thoughts into my mind, but I was not successful.

I don't remember having a moment like this. It was a feeling difficult to understand. I guess that in a sense, I was in a state of discovery about myself. My emotions. I guess women may be right when they say that men are not in touch with their feelings. Sometimes, guys can live the whole life without having to deal with their own emotions. Certainly, troubled emotions.

But some men, and I count myself among them, come face to face with strong emotions that are difficult to grasp. And we are left flabbergasted. Maybe some men have mental breakdowns at moments like that. Who knows? Maybe some people go coo-coo. I guess I react with silence. Maybe, stupefaction?

I was thankful that Hadas understood. It looked like she understood, at least.

When we neared the pyramids, I felt better. And the walking was helping as well.

"You are not going to trade me in for a few camels, are you?" Hadas looked at me and smiled. She looked absolutely radiant.

"Nope," I said, "Not for a million camels."

"How about a million and one?" Hadas joked.

"Even then, no," I said. Hadas flashed a smile that reached from her west to her east.

We walked towards where tourists rent a camel or a horse for a ride around the pyramids.

"Should we go with a horse or with a camel?" I asked.

"Definitely horses," Hadas said. "It's more romantic." As soon as she said this, she turned bright red.

"Horses, it is, then," I said.

We both hopped on a horse each and started to ride the horse on the desert floor. It felt great riding an animal in the desert scene. I felt like Lawrence of Arabia. I looked at the pyramids in the distance and felt like the Pharaoh of Egypt.

"This is the life!" I said, exulting in the experience.

"It does feel good, no?" Hadas said.

"It's more than good," I said. "It's great!" I tried to imitate Tony the Tiger from the cereal commercials, but Hadas did not get it. Maybe my imitation was bad. Maybe they don't have the same cereal commercials in Israel. Maybe it sounds different in Hebrew? Despite the curiosity, I wasn't going to ask Hadas about it. I did not want to ruin the mood of the pyramid ride.

The sun was setting and there was a red hue in the horizon.

"Simply magnificent!" I said. I took out my small digital camera and snapped some shots of the pyramids and the beautiful red horizon.

"Smile!" I said to Hadas, as I snapped her photo. Hadas smiled back and began to snap her own photos. We were engaged in a shootout of photographs, and we were laughing as the sun went down.

We circled the pyramids and thoroughly enjoyed ourselves. By the time we returned, the sun was close to complete descent.

"Shall we get some coffee?" I asked.

"Has to be Arabic coffee," Hadas said.

"Is there any other kind?" I said.

"I think, I see Starbucks over there," Hadas joked.

"Say no more," I said. "It pales to the good Arabic coffee."

We almost hopped along to the nearest Arabic restaurant, and we ordered Arabic coffee and some desert items. We were both elated and felt light-hearted.

"Wow, pyramids are definitely worth it," I said.

"Yeah," Hadas said. "I am really happy to be here."

"Me, too," I said. And we looked into each other's eyes for a moment. And instinctively, both of us started to sip the Arabic coffee in silence. It felt so right, with the sun descending and iridescent light marching across the makeshift road.

"What should we do next?" Hadas asked.

"Of course, the laser show," I said. "It's really cool. They shed differently colored lasers onto the pyramids. And the narration is quite cool, too."

"That sound good," Hadas said.

We both went to the laser show. It looked remarkably similar to the laser show in one of James Bond movies which takes place in Egypt. I wonder if the laser show changed at all in the last several decades. I guess the pyramids have been around for thousands of years, so the laser show accompanying that lasting for a few decades is not bad at all.

As we sat there watching the laser show, I put my right hand on her left hand. Her left hand seemed startled, but it did not move away. In fact, in a brief moment her hand somehow mysteriously fit into my hand like its perfect glove. I furtively threw a glance in the direction of her face. She turned and smiled. I felt like I was in peace, looking at her smile. She turned her head after a brief moment and continued to look at the laser show. I felt happy, and I also turned my gaze toward the pyramids.

I felt her left hand in my hand. It felt soft and gentle. But I felt secure as her hand firmly grasped my hand. I felt happy, and tried to remember the last time that I was this happy. I could not.

Chapter 11

I woke up next to Hadas, and I looked at her. She looked so serene and peaceful, next to me. And her face was a face of the most beautiful angel. Even in her sleep, her face was radiating. I looked at her closed eyes. Briefly, her eye lids moved as if she was dreaming something. Her face moved a bit as if she were going to wake up. I froze because I did not want her to wake up. I wanted to look at her in this beautiful state. This was the closest to what I would consider as earthly heaven. To gaze upon her face.

I lost track of time. I did not care. I felt that I could gaze at her face for hours and hours. Days and days. Weeks and weeks. Months and months. Years and years. Forever.

As I continue to look at her, I could hear the soft sound of her breathing. And I noticed the slight movement of her body as she breathed. I wanted to be a part of that breath, floating through her body. I wanted to be a part of her body, to be an integral part of it. Like that air she breathed, I wanted to be essential to her being.

I looked at her hair. They were a bit disheveled. A part of her hair fell on her forehead and on her cheeks. I looked at the

178

strands of hair that have separated from the hair mass to lie on her bare forehead and naked cheeks, and I wanted to be that hair strand. I could see that she had some split ends in her hair, but even they seemed to rest peacefully on her face, enjoying her presence. I wondered if I could touch the strands of her hair resting on her forehead and on her cheeks. I wondered if that would wake her up or not.

And I looked at her eye brows. They seemed perfectly symmetric. They were beautifully lined into a curvaceous line. I wanted to run my pointing finger gently over the eyebrows, drawing their contours. But I restrained myself, for fear that this would wake her up, and I would be deprived of looking at such angelic form for a bit longer. I could look at her like this for eternity. She looked so heavenly, that I felt that I was experience a bit of heaven on earth.

I looked at her lips. They looked a bit pouty, like she was trying to fake a protest that I was gawking at her. I quickly looked over in the direction of her eyes, and they were still closed. Relieved, I returned my gaze back upon her lips. They were slightly parted, as if she was partly breathing through her mouth. I wondered how it would be to kiss her lips at this particular moment, when she looked so angelic, like that, encompassed by all the glory of the heavenly pulchritude.

But I relinquished my desire to kiss her and indulged in the memory of the night before, when my lips locked onto her lips and tasted her lips, her succulent lips. I remembered kissing both of her lips gently in order to savor the moment. Her lips pressed slightly and slowly against my lips, and I indulged in the sensations of my affection and the bilabial tango.

I remembered gently sucking on her upper lip as if it were the tastiest candy on earth. I sucked on the right side of her lips and then the left side. Then, I moved onto more voluptuous bottom lip. And I sucked on her bottom, plump lip from the center.

I remember how as our passions heat up, we entangled our tongue with each other, trying to tie a knot without the help of our hands. Although we were ultimately unsuccessful at tying a knot, we thoroughly enjoyed the process. At moments, the passion got the better of us and our tongues took turns entering each other's mouth.

I tried to remember the sensations that occupied my mind in the elongated kissing moments as I gazed upon her lips. I felt the urge to touch her lips. Press my index finger against her plump, bottom, lower lip. To press them with my own lips. And I felt a thirst in my throat and a longing in my mouth. I could taste the taste of the kiss of the night before. And I smelled the aroma of her perfume that took hold of my nostrils.

And I looked at her ears and noticed a pierce mark on each earlobe. I remember touching her earlobes as I kissed her lips. And I remembered how her tongue entered my ear at various moments of the night past. I wondered if she derived pleasure sticking her tongue into my earlobe.

Her white neck stretched forth from those earlobes onto her shoulders. I could see that they were red all over. I remember sucking on her neck as our hands locked, the night before. I remembered the aroma of her perfume again in my nostril, even though I was far enough from her not to be able to be so consumed by the aroma. I wondered if the memory of the smell is as vivid as the memory of the sight. I wondered how long I had licked and sucked on her neck, since many places in her neck were filled with red marks of passion.

Her passion stained neck revealed her shoulders. Her skin was milky white. She had a very feminine shoulders and the wingspan of the length was not that wide at all. I remembered folding my arms behind her shoulders as we sat, body to body, facing each other, our bodies locked in a human pretzel. I felt her breathing against my face, as I pressed the left side of my face against the left side of her face. I remembered how her body made jerky motions that seemed involuntary from time to time, as her stomach pressed against my stomach. I remember holding her back with my arms pressing against her back, and running my hand through the length of her back all the way down to the top of her hips. I remember how we grasped at each other like holding onto a rope from a cliff, as if there was no tomorrow without it.

I looked at her breasts that hung from her body like beautiful boulders hanging onto a rolling Grand Canyon. I could see the smoothness of her skin on her breasts. Her nipples had a slightly pinkish, reddish hue. And it seemed to be at a flat position, almost hiding within itself, unlike the night previous, when her nipples were pointed and hard. I remember locking my lips onto her right nipples as I held her left breast in my hand. I remember running my fingers over her hardened left nipple and gently squeezing it. I remember hearing the suppressed squeal that seemed to inadvertently pop out between her closed lips.

Her breasts felt soft and alive. I remembered not being able to hold her breast in my hand for a long period as her body constantly moved and her breast slipped out of my hand. It was like a chase, my hand chasing after her runaway breast.

In contrast to the previous night, her breast seemed to be at peace. It seemed almost as if her breasts were taking a nap, too. They held steadfast and motionless in their position, hiding the nipples, which like turtles had pulled back their heads in a late morning slumber by the sunlight in a lazy beach, somewhere in the Mediterranean Sea.

One of her arms was pressing against her breast and made it look bigger than it was. Her arms looked fit, and there was a certain attractiveness about her arms that I had not noticed before. Perhaps, it was because she was lying naked before me that I could see her naked arms. Generally, a part of her arms were covered by her shirt, so it was difficult to appreciate her arms in their full glory. They looked toned. I tried to trace the curves that were subtle in her arms. Her arms looked darker against the milky white breasts. I marveled at the two different color tones that marked her body parts, so close to each other.

There was beauty that was different, but somehow the individual beauty of her arms and her breasts nicely complemented themselves to heighten her overall angelic beauty as she lay there, with her bare arm pressed against her naked breast.

I wanted to be united with that body, yet again. I wanted to feel those arms with my hands. I wanted to taste the fullness of her breasts inside my mouth, and suck on her nipples like they were lollipop filled with cherry flavor. Strong cherry flavor.

At this moment Hadas moved her body and repositioned herself. I think it was a reflex reaction and not a conscious act. When I looked at her face, she was in the same serene sleep state.

www.ingramcontent.com/pod-product-compliance
Lightning Source LLC
Chambersburg PA
CBHW022153260626
47155CB00017B/1860